THE
COLD
DOME

LINDA TEETER

PAGE PUBLISHING, INC.
Conneaut Lake, PA

First originally published by Page Publishing 2019

ISBN 978-1-64544-092-5 (pbk)
ISBN 978-1-64544-093-2 (digital)

Printed in the United States of America

Dedicated to my sisters, Elaine and Rebecca, for all their encouragement. May Jesus be glorified in this story.

Chapter One

IN THE SHADOW

I n the midst of heavy silence, the adults got up and drew together in a corner of the room. The quartet huddled together in front of the now-empty table.

Josh declared, "They're not going to let us do it. Plan B goes into action just as soon as they pull rank. Okay?" His companions nodded in agreement.

Weeks Earlier

The green door inched open with a slight hydraulic hiss. Sunlight from the morning sun blended with blond hair as a head peered around the doorjamb.

"Come on, come on!" the impatient voice of Janna urged. She stood behind Darcie, who remained rigid as she gazed past the doorway and blocked the view of those behind her.

Janna pushed Darcie aside, and two additional eager bodies squeezed through the small opening. Finally, all four teens stood in the shadow of the giant wall, speechless at the scene before them. Unnoticed, the door quietly swung back and closed with a gentle *swish*.

They stood on a narrow but paved road that ran downhill before starting to climb again. A lone mountain, with a faint blue haze hanging in the sky, stood in the distance. A handful of scrawny white barked trees stood sentinel close to the doorway. Although the trees seemed to be at odds with the cracked, baked ground they were a part of, when the wind swept across the open meadow around them, they tossed their branches into the pale-blue sky, perhaps in a desperate attempt to leave the earth holding them down.

Grasses, some green and some turning brown, joined in the dance of the wind, tossing their skinny bodies to the rhythm only they knew.

Although it was only eight in the morning, the air was warm on the explorers' skin as the breeze wrapped around their faces, kissing them before blowing off into the open spaces. Just as suddenly the breeze calmed to a gentle touch. The two fifteen-year-old girls—Darcie Manns and her best friend, Juli Turner—glanced at each other. Juli's younger siblings, thirteen-year-old twins Joshua and Janna, were uncharacteristically dumbstruck.

The leader, Darcie, oldest of the group by two months, hoisted her heavy backpack and spoke with more assurance than she felt, "Well, let's get going. We don't know how far we need to go and how long we'll have this light."

The tall shadow of their home fell on their path, and as they moved away, one by one, they couldn't help but glance back.

Darcie leafed through her notebook of memories, back to the beginning of the many secret days spent in preparation for this strange undertaking, prompted by the need for an answer to a puzzle their homeland couldn't solve.

She was a third-generation dome dweller and had spent her brief life listening to the stories of the old days that were a part of the after-supper entertainment. Her grandparents, easily persuaded to talk about the early days just before the new millennium when abortion was the law of the land, kept their audience enthralled.

They quietly told about the doctors' offices equipped with a room where anyone paid fifteen hundred dollars and received a prescription that would end whatever misery they felt they couldn't face for another day.

As a little child, she would cover her ears as horror stories told of kids killing kids in classrooms or teachers shot for assigning homework.

The theme of the story would change as the elders told how different groups drew together to maintain their way of life and continue in their beliefs against what they felt was evil.

One such group, her great-grandfather being included, arranged to lease, for two hundred years, an abandoned Army base located in the Midwest. This was an ideal location, they thought, because of the underground bunkers already in place for storage and an underground stream channeled into a deep well for inexhaustible fresh water.

Grandpa Daryl had once shown her the blueprint stored in the library that depicted how the designers had taken a dome design normally used for sporting events and adapted it to their needs, turning it into the only home she had ever known.

He proudly pointed to his father's name as one of the engineers who took a fabric form, anchored it to concrete rings for footers, inflated it with air, and sprayed it with urethane foam for insulation. Steel rebar grid-work sprayed with high-density concrete formed the walls. Most of this information went right in one of her ears and out the other.

He had marched her past the pictures on the library walls and pointed out the different phases of the work. A faraway look crossed his face as he told about the many onlookers laughing and making fun of his dad and the others. He remembered with great clarity watching as the monstrosity took shape. The planners cunningly blocked any attempts to report on what the group was building.

The workers quickly installed the cover over the frame, and all that was left for the curious was the construction sounds of machinery and workers heard both day and night, rain or shine.

Darcie's grandfather explained that all living space was designed alike: a three-story home with the sleeping areas underground, the ground room used for the kitchen and living area, and with a loft over the living room. Costs were kept to a minimum as they could buy bulk.

One of the last pictures on the library wall where they stopped was the Dome layout. Thirty percent of the Dome area designed for the greenhouses, solar-powered generators, and banks of energy-storing batteries left the balance of the area for the living quarters, the recreational sites, the factories, the food processors, and all other necessary ingredients to a healthy community.

Placed at the top of the Dome were panels to regulate the amount of sun and light needed for the inside comfort of the Dome and the maximum force needed to power the generators. Batteries stored six months of energy, keeping a comfortable atmosphere of seventy-six degrees throughout the entire dwelling. The men usually wore short sleeves all the time, and the women didn't complain too often about being cold.

Darcie read one more time the footnote that explained that the dome designed for 170,000 people to live, work, and play showed the foresight of the founding families. When they moved into the Dome, it was only 958 families, with a total population of a little more than 23,000 men, women, and children.

In sociology class, Darcie had been surprised to learn that, as the Dome attracted publicity during the building stage, an enterprising television network had made an offer of thirty million dollars to allow interviews with the people investing their funds in the construction project, including follow-up sessions at the first, fifth, tenth, twentieth, and fiftieth anniversaries. After several heated meetings, this proposal was accepted, and these funds swelled the building project. She questioned her teacher when the additional interviews had taken place. She wasn't surprised to discover they had never taken place and that, apparently, interest from the outside had been lost.

While on a trip to the other side of the Dome with her dad, Darcie had noticed one large overhead door standing alone in the wall. Amazed, she asked her dad the purpose of this lone door.

He had explained that during the building stages, this was the only egress allowed. The only time the door opened was when supplies moved in and, when the workers building the dome structure, had changed shifts.

Her dad pointed out the normal-sized house door cut into the larger one allowed any pedestrian traffic. Even now, he explained, if any out-dweller wanted to join this community, they would find an unlocked door. This unsecured opening could also be used by a dome dweller who was unable or unwilling to abide by the constitutional bylaws all had to sign.

Grandpa Joe, her dad's dad, sitting in the back of the quiet battery-operated vehicle, added that not all potential dwellers joined because of the same belief but because they were simply looking for a better way of life than what their current situation was giving them. However, they had all agreed to obey the laws written by a consensus of the founders.

He continued his lecture and explained how the planners of this new society had pored over many texts of civilizations and history where they drew on the ideals of democratic socialism and the practices of the early believers in the book of Acts, found in a book called the Bible.

No police force would control and punish wrongdoers. A panel of twelve men would review any complaint or suspected crime. If the conscience of the perpetrator forced him to give himself up or there was the testimony of at least two eyewitnesses, the panel immediately expelled the rule breaker and their family into the outside world, never to return. The community took on the needs of the offended party if no offender came forward.

The rules invoked were based on the honor system, and even children would be required to sign this pledge upon reaching the age of twelve. But for younger children, the parents would have to answer for any community crime committed by their offspring.

He added that as far as he knew, only one family had ever left the Dome; and it wasn't a part of any punishment, just a longing for things not found in the Dome yet available on the outside. Crime never became a problem, with just minor offenses disciplined by the community's rule book.

Grandpa Joe grew just a little testy as he complained about the younger generations who, bit by bit, as the community grew and as some of the early vision was lost on the current generation, seemed more tolerant of rule benders and how crime had been creeping into the fabric of the society.

He agreed that, so far, it was nothing major, just some petty theft in some of the work areas and a loss of entertainment equipment. But he scratched his head and reflected that since the economy, based on the barter system, ensured that the food supplies were free and there was no rent to pay (as the homes were purchased by the families as part of their admission to the Dome), it surely left few items to covet.

Even the burial plots, assigned deep in the catacombs under the Dome, were free. The designers had the foresight to lay out the community as a quadrant in order to spread the dwellers around the structure, allowing the growing family needing new homes to remain in the same area, if desired.

Having a captive audience as the drive continued toward home, Grandpa Joe continued on his favorite theme of their society morally declining at a fevered pitch.

He always reflected back to when each family was responsible for providing all their family's education, discipline, clothing, plus all other provisions, as well as maintaining their share of the complex.

They could barter with someone to provide for those needs, using whatever was agreeable between the parties, or assign the tasks between the family members.

But because the human spirit naturally bent for evil, it was determined to write at least some rules.

Darcie had smiled as she remembered his many comparisons to the first years of Dome living and the here and now. She often wondered if his memory didn't make those former years just a little better than they really had been.

However, that wasn't the pressing issue for the Dome dwellers, and Darcie's thoughts jumped back to her present as a strange bird swooped down close to her face.

Startled, she stared down the uncharted road, realizing that only a few seconds had passed. Her friend, Juli, standing beside her, asked again, "Are you sure you want to do this?"

Darcie turned, looking into a pair of blue eyes. Juli's blond hair pulled back from her smooth face revealed a tiny frown creasing her forehead.

Darcie's hair, also blond but with red highlights, blew into her face. Grabbing a handful, her brown eyes glaring back, she answered her friend, "You bet we're doing this! We've spent a lot of time getting ready for today."

Easygoing Juli shrugged her shoulders. "Just thought I'd ask. You're so intense over even your choice of breakfast cereal that sometimes I think you refuse to hear any voice but your own. I just don't really think this trip is necessary. Everything could work out without us doing this."

This adventure really had started just a little over two weeks ago. Juli and Darcie, walking home after listening to yet another meeting of the elders, zipped their jackets against the evening chill.

Darcie said, "Okay, so the highest temperature this year has been sixty-six degrees, and it's in the middle of summer vacation! Last year, at this time, it was seventy-four, and the year before it was seventy-six. Why isn't someone interested in finding out why it seems to be getting colder every year? All they do is talk about it. I think there is something very strange going on, and the grown-ups are trying to hide it."

"Darcie, you'd find a mystery in how the leaves fall if you tried hard enough. Although I'll admit that it is odd that no one has called a fast. The news can't even find anyone interested in giving an interview about the possible cause. Every night, as we come together, it is the topic that the entire meeting revolves around, yet no ideas have been presented. How many tests do they have to do before they find the problem?"

Darcie restated, "So wouldn't it be great if we could come up with the answer first? All the scientists agree that the amount of heat coming from the sun to the panels is the same as it was twenty-five years ago. Yet our outside temperature continues to drop, and doubling the amount of fuel doesn't keep it at seventy-six degrees like it was years ago. Nothing's coming in from the badlands because the instruments can't find any leak in the Dome."

"Why hasn't someone from the college ventured an answer? Also, although everyone agrees that the Eternal One would know the answer, no one wants to leave the comfort of home and make a trip through the badlands to find that answer."

"So no-brainer, we should go and ask him."

The first time Darcie had stated this radical plan, Juli had quickly looked up, hoping to see a twinkle in Darcie's eye and a grin on her face. Instead, Darcie had been frowning, absorbed in her thoughts; so Juli asked, "You are kidding, aren't you?"

Darcie continued walking silently, ignoring the question. Juli grabbed Darcie's arm, forcing her to stop.

"Come on, quit joking. We can't go out there. No one ever goes out there. Looking for one person in that big space is dumb. 'Sides, why should we go? Let a grown-up make the trip. We're just kids, remember?"

Juli's arguments fell to the sidewalk, unheeded, as Darcie pulled away and continued her walk, deep in thought. Later, together in the open living room, fragrant smells wafting in from the adjourning kitchen, Darcie tossed aside the textbook she had been staring at yet not reading.

Juli glanced up from her magazine, and Darcie leaned over conspiratorially.

"Look, I've got it figured out!" she whispered. "Let's go to the loft, and we can decide how much we'll need to take for clothes."

Darcie continued to muse. "Probably shouldn't take much because we'll be walking, and then we need to decide what food we can take. And oh, yeah, let's find some old books with old maps, and maybe it will show the badlands."

Still chattering away and dragging Juli reluctantly behind her, Darcie hurried upstairs to her room.

Juli kept her mouth closed and listened to the bubbling chatter. She knew that Darcie would often become excited over a cause only to totally disregard any mention of it three hours later. Juli was hopeful that Darcie's enthusiasm would soon cool after realizing that her hair dryer had no place in her backpack.

The loft, converted into Darcie's sanctuary/bedroom, was a study in contrasts. Soft green walls, with a gleaming hardwood floor, joined the white wicker bedroom furniture, revealing the talent of Darcie's mom. Yet the girls found it necessary to step over piles of clothes thrown down at random. CDs and magazines strewn over the wicker bench at the bottom of the bed increased the chaos. The dust of makeup and bottles of unknown beauty regimens covered the dresser, and underwear decorated the drawer knobs. The cornflower-colored bedclothes stood in a heap on the bed.

Darcie strode toward her desk that sat beneath the street-side window. She swept a pile of magazines from the padded seat and pushed an empty glass and pizza plate off her canvas-covered notebook. Juli, behind her, was cleaning off the bench.

Darcie said, "Well, having to go to summer learning camp is good for one thing. I don't have to hunt for pen and paper."

At the sound of running feet up the loft stairs, Darcie jumped up and exclaimed, "Quick, block the door. Don't let them in!"

Beating the twins to the door became a losing cause as the girls slipped and stumbled over the mess on the floor.

"What do you two want?" Juli growled as she turned back into the room.

"Mom wants you home. Now! You gotta clean your room."

Josh and Janna, considered by the older girls to be babies, always seemed to be underfoot. The twins, for their part, were always complaining the older teens were stuck-up.

Juli sighed. "Okay, go home, and tell her I'll be right there."

"Get your work done soon, and get back here. We've got work to do. Think of different things we'll need, and I'll add them to my list." Darcie poked her paper for emphasis.

Josh, always ready to challenge Darcie, pushed between them. "Hey, what are you guys planning now? Tell me, or I'll tell Mom you're hatching another plot."

Darcie sank down onto her chair. "This doesn't concern you two babies, and you better get out of my room before I throw you out."

"Yeah? You and what army?" retorted Josh, puffing out his chest.

"Just me! So there!" Darcie threw her pen down on the desk and jumped to her feet.

Juli, with the ease of long practice, stepped between the foes. She mildly rebuked the older girl, "Never mind that now."

Turning to her siblings, she spoke with authority, "Twins, go home. I'm right behind you. Darc, look I'll call you later, in case I can't get out. Think some more on this. You know this isn't like some of your other schemes."

With a quick hug of friendship, the girls parted; and the Turner family left for their home, which sat across the alley from the Manns' home.

Since this was lawn-mowing and sprinkling night, the air was rent by the hum of hundreds of electric motors and had the husband or brother racing to have his patch of lawn done before his neighbor. Then the balance of the night was broken by the splatter of water as the automatic systems hissed the nourishing liquid into the air, feeding the trees and grass. This was the only night of the week where everyone was required to be indoors by eight o'clock.

Absentmindedly, Darcie picked up the mess in her room as she awaited the call to supper. At six-thirty, after the nightly community meeting, the family gathered for their evening meal. Darcie, still in thought, ate her supper in near silence. Her mother questioned her health, but Darcie smiled and said she was just fine. She didn't notice the raised eyebrows between the parents. Later, as they cleaned up the meal, the mother and daughter shared some laughter, and Dad smiled to himself as he sat in his favorite chair reading the latest novel available and listening to their light chatter.

Finally, Darcie could retreat back upstairs where she grabbed her paper from her desk. Jumping on her bed and fluffing her pillows behind her, she gazed across the room, staring at the poster covered wall yet not seeing it. She pulled on her lip in concentration and furiously scribbled on her list from time to time. When the phone on the nightstand beside her rang, she quickly snatched up the receiver.

"Can you come over tomorrow night before curfew?" Darcie queried.

"Naw, I've been grounded because I was forty-five seconds late for supper, but I can talk for fifteen minutes on the phone."

Words tumbled from Darcie in her excitement. "I've been trying to remember everything I've ever heard about the Eternal One and the badlands. Boy, I wish I could get to a library. Why are the badlands a bad influence? I mean, there's a door. How come no one ever goes out or comes in? There are people out there, aren't there?"

Juli laughingly cut in, "I can't believe you actually want to go to the library. Besides, if you'd paid more attention in class and less on Joel Evans, you'd remember the video they showed of what the badlands were like."

"No, I remember that day well. I was passing notes to Joel and ended in isolation, and then his mom grounded him. So I never saw the movie. Anyhow, I thought that was just something they used to scare us to never go outside the Dome."

Juli rebuked, "Darcie Manns, you're impossible. Well, they said it took three years to make this movie because all they had were old pictures. I still have bad dreams about all that open space. There are miles out there without a house in sight, and there didn't seem to be any place to eat."

Juli shuddered as she remembered. "They simulated what could happen if someone tried surviving out there. According to the computer theory, anyone would break down mentally as their body and mind would be assaulted by loneliness and temptations."

She warmed to her topic. "I think you're absolutely crazy to even think this, and I don't think I'm going!"

"Oh, is that right? I am not crazy! I'm offering you an adventure that isn't even against the law. Perhaps the real reason you won't go is fear of the unknown. You're so afraid of anything unexpected that you'll let your best friend go alone."

"Oh, Darcie, don't be so mean. Just remember all the other things you've dragged me into and all the restrictions I've gotten because of you." Juli, pleading, sought to convince her friend. "Who knows how long we'd be gone, and what could we tell our parents? How could we survive out there with no food?"

Juli sighed into the phone. "I still want to be your friend, but I don't want to get into any more trouble."

"Well, I've already solved most of our problems. I've got the perfect scheme," Darcie gleefully replied. "You know dome maintenance camp is starting next week and every year we hear how we should go and we always find some excuse to stay here and do our thing. Now it is ideal. We'll tell the parents that we'll go this year. It's for a month and two hundred miles away on the other side the city. They'll be so surprised and glad they will even help us pack for our trip."

"So we're going to lie to our parents about where we're going, and that's supposed to make me feel better? What happens if our trip takes more than a month? We'll worry them to death. What kind of example is that for the kids we have to mentor?" Even as Juli was taking another breath and trying to marshal more arguments against Darcie's scheme, her bedroom door burst open and the twins exploded into Juli's room.

"We're going too!" squealed Janna, dragging the phone from Juli's ear and shouting into the receiver.

"Going where?" asked Juli innocently, "And let me have the phone back."

"You know where," snickered Josh. "We're going with you into the badlands. What fun!"

Darcie hollered into the phone, "What's going on?"

Juli grabbed the receiver back. "Instead of being in bed like they were supposed to, the twins were outside my door, apparently listening."

Janna lowered her voice and said, "We're going or I'll tell about your little scheme and then you'll get it."

Juli groaned and told Darcie of the threat and added, "She will, you know, and we'll be grounded for at least the rest of the summer. And who knows what else they'll dream up to punish us. It's not like it's the first time we've been in trouble!"

Then, changing her thought process, Juli mused, "Yet if it's dangerous, none of us should go. Otherwise, let's take them."

At this abrupt reversal from Juli, Darcie questioned, "What's going on? You were giving me such a hard time, and now, suddenly, it's okay?"

On the other end of the phone, Juli remained silent for a moment. "I don't know. It's just that I got a feeling that it is okay. I just wish we didn't have to lie."

Darcie, not wanting to rock the boat and tip Juli back onto timid ground, told her, "So let's not tell a total lie. Let's get our trip done quickly and really go to camp. We'll just be about a week later than the rest. I still think if we get the answer, no one will care about our little deception."

"As far as the twins are concerned, we'll take them along. Josh can be a help, but tell them they had better keep up. We won't wait for babies."

The next day, the four conspirators held their first planning session. The loft became campaign headquarters where Darcie whipped her smudged, wrinkled list from the back pocket of her jeans and spread it out on her bed. She sent Janna after a couple of books from the encyclopedia set.

She told Josh, "Go find a copy of the camper's guide, and read up on cooking over something other than a stove, if that's possible, and how we can sleep without a roof over us. You went to that male retreat last year, so how did you guys sleep outside? And I always wanted to ask, why did you sleep outside? Anyhow, can you borrow enough sleeping bags for all of us without anyone getting suspicious? There's lots of stuff we need to know."

Josh frowned and said, "The only guide I know of is the old copy Dad has, and that's so old it's yellow and stinks. Will that do?"

Darcie nodded. "That's okay. Nobody goes camping anymore, so it'd have to be old."

Josh banged into Janna as she entered with two large books spilling from her arms. The girls flipped through the pages, and Darcie made notes.

"I guess most of the stuff we need to read about outside the Dome was destroyed in that accident we had in the archives five years ago 'cause most of this was written by a professor here at the college. So he's never been outside either, but he says that the badlands does have food and water. We just don't know much about where they are and what they are. Let's hope we can find some stores or restaurants rather than finding berries along the way."

Janna, her sandy-colored braids hanging over the book she had on the floor, piped up and asked, "What's the wildlife he talked about?"

"I don't know, Sis. Maybe it's a type of food."

Again, the cautious Juli questioned Darcie, "Are you sure this is a good idea? I mean, do we really care about whether the temperature is changing in here? Maybe we really should attend the maintenance camp and forget this."

Darcie shook her head vehemently. "Not on your life. I bet Susan Fogget a whole month's allowance that I could find the Eternal One, and I'm going."

Juli bounced up from the floor, hands on her hips, and glared. "You made a bet on this? Boy, you really bug me!"

With a lopsided grin, Darcie sheepishly explained, "Well, she called last night right after I got off the phone with you, and the topic just happened to come up. I didn't tell her everything, just that we were going to find the answer everybody wants. I swore her to secrecy, but now I'll go, just for spite." She paused pensively. "But it's like I'm being drawn outside—to something wonderful."

As Josh came back into the room, he snorted. "Now who's day-dreaming? Tell me, how can you prove that you found the Eternal One? Gonna bring him home with you? I think you're just being drawn to something that will get you attention."

Darcie ignored the slight and enthusiastically threw her hands in the air. "Don't you see? That's the beauty of my plan! Think about it. We find him, get the right answer, bring it back, and tell my dad. Since he's an engineer, he can tell the people, and they will listen. Knowing Dad, he'll give us credit, and I figure we'll be famous with our names on the news. And maybe they'll decide to give us a reward, and there will be enough money that I can get that Z534 car I've been dying for. Fame, fortune, and respect! Sure, I wouldn't mind a little attention, and this can get it for us. And it wouldn't even take much work on our part."

Chapter Two

THE BADLANDS

Using every possible excuse to be together, Darcie would call a secret meeting. She handed out assignments, and each person would huddle over books, DVDs, and maps. Slowly, she watched a scheme develop with careful planning.

Juli reminded everyone that it was important that all used the same story. She planned the provisions for the trip by having everyone filch a little from each meal. She told Josh to use the excuse that he was growing and needed more food. He made and stashed extra sandwiches, moving them into the food backpack little by little.

Finally, the night before the adventure was to start, Darcie called one last meeting. She held the list and called off the items as Juli double-checked everything spread across the loft's floor.

Before it had been of any use, a spilled pop ruined the thin campers' guide Josh had found. Any attempt to separate the pages while wet resulted in total destruction. Even after the pages dried, the brittle book fell apart with the slightest turning of a page. So Darcie knew their list was incomplete but hoped it would be adequate for their needs.

Not much sleep was forthcoming for Darcie that night as she tossed and turned, wondering if they would really pull this off and what was beyond the soon-to-be-opened door.

The following morning, the four teens waved as the two electric cars carried their unsuspecting parents homeward. No comments had even been made by their parents about the stuffed backpacks they all carried. A curve took the cars out of sight, and Darcie motioned the others onto the roadway. They turned their faces to the site of the door.

No passerby stopped them or spoke a word of caution as they neared the door that would open up an unknown world of adventure.

Moments later, they stood outside, in the shadow of their home, reluctant to take the first step away from what they knew.

Janna was the first to notice and exclaim, "Hey, the Dome has scenery painted up as high as I can see. How come we never noticed?"

"We probably did, but it didn't mean anything then. Now that we see the real badlands, you can tell," her brother answered.

Then he asked, "Did they paint so we couldn't see out or so no one could see in?"

Juli, still staring around, commented, "It's so green and so blue and so…what is this strange air moving the grass around? I like it, yet it has so much more life than the breeze created by our fans."

Nervously, she chattered on, "How can anyone stand it for long? Maybe we'd better go back. I'm not sure this can work. I'm getting a headache. It's so bright. We'll probably go blind before we can find the Eternal One."

Clapping her hands with glee, Janna, always ready for an adventure regardless of the consequences, exclaimed, "I think this is just great. Don't you, Josh? Come on, you old scaredy-cats. What's a little bright light? We'll get used to it. Come on!"

Josh, taller than Janna by half an inch, took a deep breath and started moving away from the Dome toward the solitary, distant blue mountain that seemed painted on the sky. As the only boy, with his advice and input often ignored by the girls, he still quickly jumped to their defense when needed. It was okay for him to tease but just let someone else at the Center try.

Juli and Darcie looked at each other and then pushed past the twins, with Darcie saying, "We're leading this trip! We aren't afraid either. Just enjoying this beauty, something you unwashed wouldn't know about."

She directed the party of four down the broken road where, hopefully, at the end of it, they could find the Eternal One. Most of the books they had read were very vague on who he was or where he was. One article had stated that he was everywhere and would answer anyone who called his name. Josh had stated that seemed too easy, so they agreed to reject that theory.

Yet another said that he would answer you only after you proved yourself worthy of his attention. That portrayed more realistically the life the young people experienced, so that was the article Darcie decided they would use to glean their information.

The author of that article stated that he had never had a "mountaintop experience," but he quoted from many old manuscripts that talked of men "climbing up"; so he would not ignore the possibility. Based on that idea, Janna found some old maps and searched for the location of the mountains nearest the Dome. Hoping any mountain would work, she pointed to the lonely mountain that now seemed to be at the end of the road. The map had also shown mountains on the other side of what looked like a large body of water the map called an ocean. Not even Janna mentioned the obvious fact that none of the books gave any clear indication where the searchers could locate the Eternal One's home.

As they walked, Darcie and Juli continued their ongoing discussion about the Eternal One. The more research they had read about this all-knowing grown-up, the less seemed understandable. All the different authors had their own picture of what he was like. Some said he was gentle and loving; some wrote of anger and punishment; and others depicted him as aloof and unconcerned about mankind's problems. Yet all the authorities they read agreed this Eternal One had all the wisdom of the world and would share it just for the asking.

Josh had asked his parents, after one of the nightly meetings, "Why aren't our leaders asking him for the answers for all our problems?"

He received only vague answers of "old wives' tales" and "superstitious nonsense that doesn't apply today." All the grown-ups in Josh's life seemed reluctant to address this solution. Now, every nightly meeting he attended, the people were totally occupied with the problem but offered no concrete solution, and certainly, the choice of asking for help from an unknown source was not offered.

So it was truly an uncharted route the four teens were now traversing—a route any adult seemed unwilling to choose.

The air outside the Dome was heavy with the smell of the flowers growing in the ditch off the road, and insects buzzed by their ears.

Juli pondered aloud, "Doesn't it seem to be noisier out here yet quieter at the same time? It sounds like hundreds of birds are singing, but I've only seen a couple flying overhead. There are no motors buzzing, people talking, and kids screaming as they play."

She continued, "It truly is a different world. The colors, the smell—everything seems so much more alive than what we have. Look at the grass bend as if it's alive and wants to dance. Look at those clouds moving, something we only read about in our books. They're fluffy and white, and that one looks like a kitten. I never knew the sun could be so bright and hot. Where's the temperature control out here? It's too much to take in."

Still chattering, she moved off toward their distant goal. Although the road that stretched in front would look smooth, it always remained broken and chipped with sharp grass pushing up through the cracks and small pebbles resting on top to roll under her feet, making the footing treacherous.

The early morning hours passed, and the sun climbed higher in the blue sky. Janna's feet, unused to much walking, became sore, and her legs grew tight. She experienced for the first time in her young life, an uncontrollable heat that beat down on her uncovered head and complained about the sweat that ran freely down her cheeks and under the backpack straps.

Juli needlessly pointed out that the always-available public transportation and the level air temperature of the Dome hadn't come with them on this trip.

Encouraging the weary foot soldiers, Darcie pointed down the road and said, "We'll stop for rest at the first tree we find that will give us shade. I don't know who planned this road, but they could have planted some trees from time to time. Stopping at any of those forests over there would probably add a whole hour to our trip, and

I don't want to leave this road. As long as we're on it, we can always find our way home. But can you believe this? All this open area, and no houses, no people, no restaurants, plus hardly any shade since we left the door and not even a park. It's kind of spooky. Is there anyone out here except us?"

The trip continued, and shortly after Janna complained for the third time about being tired, hungry, and thirsty, a casting shadow across the road caused Josh, in the lead, to notice it first.

Walking wearily with her head down, the thrill of all the beauty surrounding her gone with the onset of fatigue, Juli just concentrated on placing one foot in front of the other, making sure she missed the trip hazards always in the path and not wishing to see that the mountain never seemed closer.

Josh glanced up when the cooler air hit his brow. He stopped in his tracks. "Look here!"

The girls, a few steps behind, dutifully stopped and looked.

"It looks like a Christmas tree except it's green," giggled Janna. "What a silly color for it, and what a silly place for it to be in the middle of summer."

Juli pushed by her saying, "Well, maybe, but the temperature is probably ten degrees cooler over here than where you are. Come on, Darcie, it must be time to break out those sandwiches. I'm eating, drinking, and then taking a nap. Man, I didn't realize I was this out of shape."

Her pack thudded to the ground, and everyone quickly shed their backpacks too.

Darcie flopped onto the needle-carpeted ground and hunger pains prompted her to forage inside her pack.

Not only was she the eldest but she also was tallest, so she was carrying the biggest backpack, where the food was stored, with just enough room for a few clothes. She would need a Laundromat every couple of days to clean her couple of pairs of jeans and light tops, but the food was more important.

During the assigning of jobs, Josh had tried to exercise his masculine role and claim the right to carry the all-important food bag. If Juli, the peacemaker, hadn't worked a compromise and talked Darcie into letting Josh carry the water bottles and the latrine equipment, the battle might have turned physical and the bag ripped in two. Now if Darcie's aching shoulders were regretting having won that right to carry the heaviest pack, pride kept her mouth closed.

Temporarily sating their hunger, comfortable positions were sought on the unyielding ground, and one by one, using their packs as pillows, they dozed off.

Yet even the physical weariness couldn't overcome the stones digging into Juli's back, the biting of the insects that Josh tried to fend off, and the cramping of Darcie's calves, so the naps were shorter than desired, although they seemed refreshing.

Janna sipped from her canteen again as Darcie reminded everyone to hoard the water until a new supply appeared.

Joshua took his shovel and the curtains and rods he carried and set up their first experience with an open-air bathroom. The girls had been horrified to read that campers had to build their own latrines. Juli could not accept the fact that there would not be four walls and privacy, so Josh earned many brownie points when he designed a series of pipes he would pound into the dirt and slide window curtains onto connecting rods that sat down into this piping system, forming a shower-curtain effect around a hole dug into the dirt. Juli made sure she carried many packets of tissue, and she doled them out conservatively. Josh would set up and tear down his invention at every rest stop that did not provide a normal bathroom.

Feeling a little more enthusiastic about the trip and seeing that the mountain was surely a little closer, Darcie turned her face west and motioned the group back onto the road, continuing the trek toward the mountain.

Juli would veer off the path from time to time and pluck a handful of ruby-red wild roses and bright-yellow black-eyed Susans that grew so abundantly along the roadside. She soon had a wreath woven and placed on her head. It made her look even more attractive as her blue eyes were a contrast to the bright red blended into her golden hair.

Josh mentioned that the land, at first glance, seemed completely flat between the Dome and the far distant mountain but was changing as the miles paced by. Shrubs became trees, and the flat ground gave way to gentle swells that grew steeper and harder to climb. The road curved first one way and then back again, as if whoever had laid out the path was determined not to make it straight.

He puffed out, as he reached the top of yet another slope, "This is probably what the dictionary called a hill. Remember? It said that a mountain was higher than a hill. Just think of what that mountain will be like to climb! I think we're on pace for doing our goal of three miles an hour and should be in the area within the three days we have available."

Hills and miles later, Josh reached the top of the steepest hill yet and paused in surprise. The road just stopped, and only some parched shrubs and sharp-looking rocks stood in their path. But that wasn't the real surprise. Down below, hidden until he had crested the hill, sat a town and farms stretching away into the valley as far as he could see. Across the open gorge, on the other side, he could see where the paved road returned. The only way to get there would be to go down the valley and up the other side.

Astonished at the sight, Darcie motioned them off the path and into the bushes, standing guard at the crest of the hill, hoping no watcher or sentinel had spotted them silhouetted against the late-afternoon sky. She breathed, "So there are people still out here."

She inwardly winced as three sets of eyes solemnly stared at her. Without them saying a word, she knew they were asking the question "What should we do?" She gave herself a mental shake. This was a test of leadership. Leaders must be decisive, and if they were unsure, their followers should never know it. But she could ask herself a million questions, such as should they retrace their steps and find a way around this possible menace, or strike off boldly into the unknown? She would have to decide and quickly.

Trusting her instincts, she reached her decision and said, "Let's go down there. I think it'd be neat seeing how these people live. We'll assume they're just like us but with different customs."

There seemed to be one main road stretching the length of the small town. As she scanned for activity below that would give her a clue about the inhabitants, she squinted against the flash of sunlight bouncing out of the low cloud bank just touching the top of the hill opposite the one where they crouched.

One end of the town had nice houses and taller buildings of some kind, but the opposite end, the end farthest from their sight, looked like a war zone. A lone steeple stood above the rubble in the surrounding street. Buildings had only a back wall still standing, with the front level to the ground and side walls that pitched jagged spikes into the sky. What a strange town, or perhaps two towns that ran together; it certainly looked like two different worlds within a stone's throw of each other.

The farms lying before her, just outside of the town, sported animals of various shapes, with fields sown in straight lines of little green shoots poking out of the rich-looking brown dirt. The field before them stood in the middle of lush green trees and closely growing bushes, with green pastures setting a backdrop.

Darcie finally waved her hands toward the left of the path and said, "Josh, go ahead a little ways, and see if you can find a quiet street we can use. Let's not stroll down their main drag advertising that we're strangers until we know more about them. Maybe they have rules and restrictions that'll get us into so much trouble we can't get to the mountain."

Sounding a lot braver than she felt, Darcie, prompted by curiosity that outweighed caution, moved herself into action. Stretching before them was something that the books couldn't tell them. *Besides,* she reasoned to herself, *what danger could there be that we can't hide from?* All the hours they had walked during this first day away from home were uneventful, with no sign of danger or harm and certainly no civilization until now.

However, some self-preservation instinct made the quartet take advantage of all the foliage of the bushes and hollows offered by the land as Josh picked the path that would lead them to town.

He carefully skirted them around patches of gravel that would roll under their feet and motioned them around a thorny bush that reached out to grab a piece of their shirt or shorts.

Finally, they entered the outskirts, and Darcie grouped them all in the mouth of an alleyway at the edge of the first dwellings.

"You guys stay here. I'll look in some of their stores and check out their houses. If I'm not back in fifteen minutes, Juli, get the kids out of here and head for home. Tell my dad what happened."

Janna's mouth started puckering, and tears sprang into her eyes. Although she fought with everyone, she also loved them all deeply. "Darcie, don't go! I don't want anything happening to you. Can't we all go, or can't we all get out of here?"

Juli agreed. "Yes, we should stick together. We started together, and what happens, happens to all. Besides, how could we tell your dad that we left you?"

Darcie didn't argue. She could be brave, but companionship made it easier. So she laid out a simple reconnaissance plan.

Leaning against the cold brick wall at the mouth of the alleyway, Darcie peered around the corner.

Again, the paved street had holes, but the holes in the pavement were smaller, and there appeared to be some plan to keep them from becoming the size of the craters found in the road outside of town. Stripes separated the road into two lanes, and vehicles were moving past one another at a sedate pace.

These vehicles didn't look or sound like the ones used in the Dome. There was no gentle hum. In fact, a very large, heavy transport of some type roared by just as Josh peeked around Darcie's arm. A black trail of smoke came from a stack on its front hood, leaving an odor in the air they had never smelled before.

"Wow," Josh exclaimed, "what is that monster? And does it stink!"

After watching the stream of traffic for a few minutes, Darcie decided, "Let's just wander down this street like we belong. In other words, Josh, quit gawking! These buildings don't look like ours, but I'll bet they're for living in and some are for businesses. After all, the whole universe needs shelter and a way to earn a living."

When you didn't know what would step out of the doorway you were approaching or what would be waiting around the next blind corner, it was hard to walk casually. By silent consent, Josh took the lead.

The streets and sidewalks were much like home, but some of the buildings arose stories and stories above the ground and would have been in danger of brushing the top of the Dome if built there. A few of the cars passing by ran down under some of those tall buildings and seemingly swallowed whole.

What looked to be motorized bicycles buzzed by, sounding like angry bees, weaving in and out of traffic with seemingly little regard for any rules. Janna, glancing down other alleyways as she passed by, pointed out the swirls of paintings all over the walls, some just with words and some with designs.

She exclaimed, "Boy, would we be in trouble at home for doing that!"

Smells, sounds, and strangeness continued to assail all her senses. It was hard to look and walk without stumbling over the uneven sidewalk and still look like she was just a part of the jostling crowd.

Darcie's astonishment grew and grew until finally, as she passed the first plate-glass store window, all her rules were forgotten. Here before her feasting eyes was an array of clothing in all different colors and shapes.

She whispered to Juli, "Everyone around us is wearing such strange clothes. You can't tell where they work because nothing's the same. They're all different colors—not just denim shirts and shorts. They aren't even wearing their good clothes. I think we could be in trouble. We might as well be wearing signs that say we don't belong here."

Josh leaned in and whispered back, "Maybe I can go in one of these stores and get us some clothes like theirs?"

"I don't think so, Josh. I have a feeling that what we brought for bartering won't work here." Juli, their treasurer, thrust her hand into her pocket.

"Let's just go into this alley, circle back, and leave the same way we came. We need to get into the hills on the other side. We're starting to lose the light of the day. See, their streetlights are coming on."

No one objected to Juli's suggestion, and Janna drew closer to her older sister, groping for her hand.

"Hey, what are you kids doing out after curfew?"

The authority in the voice speaking angrily behind them froze Darcie and her companions in their tracks, and she felt an icy finger run down her spine. She knew she should turn around, but the fear immobilized her.

Beside her, Juli improvised, "Uh, sorry, sir. I guess we just weren't watching the time. We're sorry, really. We'll get home now."

Darcie felt a tug on her arm, and the girls moved away. Yet the voice halted them again.

"Say, that's cute. You're all dressed the same. What kind of summer school are you in anyhow? None of the local schools require uniforms."

The voice paused and then continued, "I'll bet you kids aren't from around here, are you?"

Chapter Three

THE DISCUSSION

A long, anguished moment went by, and Josh felt he could hear wheels and gears turning in the man's head. Boldly turning for the first time toward the source of the voice, Josh saw only an angry grown-up standing in the mouth of the alleyway. The man looked like them, except for his clothes.

Like his father, this man's hair, streaked with gray, was neatly trimmed. Unlike his father who wore only gray, befitting his station, this man wore brown pants and had a yellow shirt tucked into his belt. Some type of soft rounded cap with a bill at the front covered his head.

Darcie quickly gripped Janna's shoulder, knowing that, even in this situation, she would have questions trembling on her lips, threatening to burst out.

"So you're not from here, and you're all dressed the same. Hmm…" The stranger paused. "Let me think."

Again, he watched and waited, but the huddled teens stood silent before him. The man rubbed his chin and suddenly snapped his fingers.

"I know all the schools to the south. There aren't any schools to the west anymore, and the closest town to the north was just emptied of the people because of the poisoned water system. So that leaves the east. But there aren't any towns out there because the road dead-ends at that place called the Dome. No one is even sure that anyone is still alive in there. Is that where you're from?"

Darcie dug her elbow into Janna's side as she started to nod.

The stranger caught the motion, and with a smile at Janna, he clapped his hands together. "I can't believe my luck! This is unreal! What could possibly bring you out of there into the real world?"

He quickly glanced down the street behind him and then his face turned pleasant and his voice friendly. Unexpectedly, Darcie felt tempted to tell the whole story.

Even as she hesitated, Josh, ever trusting, broke into excited speech, "How come you know where we're from, and we don't know a thing about you? What's the name of this place?"

Encouraged by her twin's boldness, Janna questioned, "Why do you wear such funny clothes?"

Grabbing each by the arm, Juli commanded, "Be quiet, you two! I'm sorry, sir. Sometimes they forget their manners."

She glared their protestations into silence. "Well, if you'll excuse us, we'd better get going and get home." She threw her arms around the twins' shoulders and again tried to brush past the man blocking their way.

The man had been grinning at Juli's interaction with the young questioners, but as the children moved to skirt him, he quickly responded by moving in front of them again, continuing to block the mouth of the alley. He held up his hands.

"Hold on a minute! We all know you're not going home. So just where do you think you're spending the night? This city has a curfew for good reason. And if caught, you'll be tossed into a dorm and will be spending a lot of time explaining who you are. They'll split you up into several different foster homes until they decide your cases."

He watched as they exchanged glances, letting his words sink in, and then continued, "Perhaps you should consider coming home with me, at least for tonight. After dark, the only people on the street are not the kind you take home to meet your parents. It is dangerous, and I couldn't rest knowing you were out here. Besides, your options of where to spend the night are really limited to the streets or those hills, if you can get there before complete darkness hits. However, I can get you to my house without trouble, but we have to go now."

Seeming to take their acceptance for granted, he began walking away, calling back over his shoulder, "Come on! The law or a gang could show up at any time."

The travelers needed a quick decision.

Darcie nodded but didn't move.

Juli frowned at the ground and didn't move.

Josh followed the stranger without hesitation.

Janna said, "I hope he feeds us," as she followed Josh. The two older girls glanced at each other and then hurried to catch up.

Their new acquaintance moved away with long strides, glancing often at the red sky that was quickly growing dark. He led them further into the small city and increasingly closer to the area that looked like a war zone. Buildings, standing tall and well lighted, abutted buildings with no glass left in their windows and doors hanging on one hinge.

Their guide constantly glanced over his shoulder, and his eyes were always on the move. The travelers became more and more apprehensive as the few streetlights still available were dim from the dirty bulbs or dark from missing bulbs. The sidewalk disappeared, and they shared the road with a few passing vehicles. Finally, at the end of the last block that had a sole streetlight still shining, the man turned into a brick building and climbed a dark flight of stairs.

Janna, who was following on his heels, felt the wall for a railing to help guide her in the dim light. Feeling something cold and wet on the wall, she quickly withdrew her hand and wiped it on her shorts. Before she could warn the others, she heard her companions grunt behind her as they also groped for something to give them a sense of peace going up into this dark hole and found slime instead.

At the landing above them, their guide threw a switch, and dim light filtered down. Janna could then see that along the wall beside her hand was green mold growing in patches. Damp wallpaper hung in strips, and the tread under her feet was broken with one step loose and hanging out to trip the unaware.

Calling down to the travelers to hurry, the man inserted a key and stepped back to usher them into a small hallway. They passed two closed doors and entered an untidy room with a few pieces of furniture—some familiar, some not.

Yellowed wallpaper with a vine pattern, too faded to tell the original color of the pattern, covered the walls. The carpeting, while wall-to-wall, was bare in spots with old stains showing near the couch from long-forgotten spilled drinks. They watched as their guide placed a board between two wooden brackets and secured the door. He turned.

"Welcome to my humble home. It's small, but it's mine. Now, I know you have some questions, and believe me, I have some too. But let's fix a meal first and discuss this with full stomachs. I'll rustle up something in the kitchen. The john is to the left of the entry door, and the TV's over there."

He disappeared into the other room with the closed door, and Janna complained, "What kind of language does he speak? I can't understand what he's saying. Who is John, and why is he in the other room and can't come out? Why does he call a VP a TV? He kept talking about a school—what's that? Where's the video? This room is so small. That is one ugly couch. What's a curfew? And he's dressed so…I vote we get out of here—just as soon as we eat. You don't think he'd poison us, do you?"

Josh, leaping to his new friend's defense, shushed her. "Keep your voice down. He seems friendly enough!"

Responding to some of Janna's flow of excited words, Juli said, "A curfew is a restriction on being outdoors. I don't know how we'll know if he's telling the truth. So, I think we're stuck for the night." She sighed and added, "I'd rather be home in my own bed."

While she was speaking, Josh moved back down the hall to the other closed door but returned shortly with a broad grin and the noise of running water in the room he'd left.

"The john is just a bathroom." He faced his twin. "Boy, quit bellyaching. Where's your sense of adventure? Besides, don't you trust me to take care of you?"

Flouncing onto the overstuffed couch that dominated the small room, Janna sat in a sulk at her twin's criticism. The other girls disappeared into the bathroom.

The rattling of dishes and fragrant smells issued from the room where the stranger had disappeared. Josh fiddled with the knobs on the TV and got sound and picture. He quickly turned it off as forbidden images filled the screen on every channel he selected.

"Boy, the parents would have a fit if they found us watching a video like this. But I don't see how to change it. There's just this wire running out the back of this gadget and up the wall. I don't even see where he stores his videos. Sure is a strange place."

The call for dinner was impatiently awaited by the hungry stomachs that been filled, oh so long ago, by just a few PBJ sandwiches. Janna kept her arms pressed against her stomach to quell the growls.

Finally, their host stuck his head around the corner and invited them into the room where the good smells awaited. A table and four chairs dominated the middle of the room where counters lined one wall, with a refrigerator and stove on the adjoining wall. Cupboards ran up over the sink, and a clock stood over the doorway.

"It's just fish and chips. I hope that's all right."

Janna and Josh shared one of the hard chipped, painted metal chairs, and it was with thinly disguised impatience that they waited for their host to sit down.

"Go ahead, dig in. You do eat fish, don't you? It seems that I remember reading that you don't have beef in there but plenty of trout in your stream." He beamed around the table at them. His smile was soon replaced by a look of concern. "What's wrong?"

"When there's an adult present, we wait for them to bless the food. That's the law," Darcie stated.

Their host, taken aback, said, "What's blessing the food?"

Janna wrinkled her face up. "It's, you know, saying thanks for the food."

"Who are we thanking? There's no one here but us, and I provided the food. Just tell me thank you, and let's eat."

The quartet exchanged glances.

Darcie said, "Sounds fair. No one ever explained why we do that. It's just what we always do. So thank you!"

Mouths quickly filled left little time to be devoted to conversation. Darcie kept an eye on their host who was waiting but with little-concealed impatience. After the meal, she assigned everyone a task; and soon the emptied and dirty plates, washed and put away, removed the conversation barrier. She herded the others after their benefactor into the living room and watched as everyone found a place to sit on the pillows, the floor, or the couch.

Finally, the stranger opened up the dialogue. "Although I make my living as a guide taking people hunting and fishing in the nearby mountain, my real interest is past civilizations. I probably have the most complete records short of the museum. I'm currently working on a paper about the time just after the social breakup and the culture shock that arose as a result.

"Everyone was sure they had the answer for the perfect society, and different leaders were springing up all over. Poverty, sickness, famine, and crime had gotten so bad that the population was ripe for any scheme that gave them hope. About the only one that survived past the planning stage was the Dome.

"It must be kismet that I was the one who spotted you kids. What freshness you'll bring my report, and I could contact the TV networks who would bid big bucks to get you on their shows first. One network had even arranged for interviews with the Dome dwellers after they had been there for a while but never followed up because of all the other things that demanded reporting after those people moved into the Dome. Then, I think, we just forgot."

Darcie paid more attention when she heard the words "big bucks." Although not sure what that was, the connotation seemed financial, and she could relate to that.

"Excuse me, sir, but we don't even know your name." She could be very polite around adults when it suited her purpose.

He laughed, "Yes, I'm sorry. My mind was filled with so many other things I forgot my manners. My name is Philip Conner, but you can just call me Con. And what are your names?"

Darcie pointed and introduced each, finishing with herself. "I really don't think we can stay longer than tonight since we're on an important mission for the Dome. Maybe we can come back later and stay a couple of days. We're hoping to receive a big reward when we get back, so maybe we can work something out with you too."

Juli, attempting to catch Darcie's eye, realized that once again, Darcie was purposefully ignoring the signals.

Philip stared curiously at Darcie. "A mercenary Dome kid? Everything I've ever read indicated this was a society discouraging gain. I thought everyone had the same things and that it didn't matter what job you did, doctor or chimney sweep, you all had the same standard of living."

Embarrassed, Juli broke in ahead of Darcie, "Forgive her, sir. That is very true or was up until the last few years. Lately, some of the young rulers think that is all wrong. They want more rewards if they are doctors and not just a store clerk or something that doesn't take special training. Darcie has been reading some of their forbidden tracts, and I'm afraid she's all for it."

"Hey, maybe it was OK at first to have everyone sharing everything, but that was their choice. No one is giving us that same choice. When I get my job, I'd like to get paid more if I do more, that's all." Darcie's face turning a little red, she faced away from Juli and leaned toward Philip.

"Did you know there was a society that for over two hundred years, operated on capitalism? You could change your job at will. You could decide your pay and all other kinds of good things. That's what we want."

Philip, noting the expression on Darcie's face, hastily said, "I think I would have to agree with her myself. Money is the main reason I stay working as a guide, and luckily, I could get it. Yet look at where I'm living. You can easily understand why I'd like to make more. I want nicer things. That's what life's all about.

"I've heard of that society too. The trouble was they got lazy and wanted their government to do everything for them. They willingly gave up their freedom to be guaranteed health care, a job, and retirement. Once that happened, the example the world had for democracy disappeared, and history teaches it was only a generation later that turned this into what you see out my window. Remember that before you try changing what you have."

Sensing he had made some points with their leader, he now turned his attention to Juli in a placating attempt. "I hope you won't think me so caught up in making a living that I don't appreciate the concept the founders of the Dome had. To create a society where everyone could be truly equal and, then, best of all, actually achieve it, is a dream that's been around for as long as mankind. However, I'm frankly amazed that it's lasted so long. It sure hasn't for any other place that tried. Out here, after the civil war and having the central government close down, it's been every section for itself."

Josh broke in, "There was a civil war after we moved into the Dome?"

Philip Conner nodded. "Sure was. About five years after your ancestors shut the door, things got real tense. The courts in the old legal system were making rulings not liked by many people who had stayed outside of the Dome. Hate-speech laws passed without voters' consent. Arrests were made of the leaders who fought this new society. One thing led to another, and finally, the government just declared war on those religious terrorists. Some areas became real hotbeds of terrorist activities. Any time those acts were found, like praying in public or having meetings together, the government would call in planes, tanks, and bombs in an attempt to shut down this illegal activity. This area where we are was a war zone for most of the war, and as you saw, our buildings remain in ruins. We just don't have the manpower, money, or desire to fix them. We just make do with what we have.

"Law enforcement is nil after dark, and gangs sneak in from the southern hills. No one is safe on the streets, hence the curfew. We'll lose a few animals out on the pastures from time to time, and our stolen crops lead to rationing.

"Perhaps we can learn things from you guys that will help our situation out here. It's every man fighting for anything he can get, and many feel that's not the plan we should have. I'm not convinced of your solution, but the way your people have stuck together and supported one another show that it might help out here."

Juli held her peace, and Philip was unsure whether he had appeased her. Darcie, finding the attention drawn away from her and her importance as the leader, moved restlessly. Philip immediately returned to his campaign of convincing Darcie to meet his need.

"So what are you bringing back for the Dome that could be so important? I didn't think they had any needs unsolved."

Darcie hesitated, uncertain how much she could share before this adult laughed or, worse, forbade them to go on.

"Before I tell you that, please tell us what you know of the history of the Dome. All we're taught are the rules that we must obey, and no one talks about, or maybe doesn't know anymore, the background on why our ancestors moved in there and didn't remain out here like you. A lot of our records, destroyed in a fire we had, only left us with old memories, so we don't have much actual information. In fact, they prefer that we never ask questions about the badlands. We have one door that allows us access to the badland. And they don't lock the door, but no one ever leaves. Is there some big secret?"

Philip Conner beamed at her. "I'd be happy to tell you the history of your world as I know it. Let me get a drink, and I'll tell you what I've learned in my research. Anybody else want something?"

While he was in the kitchen, Juli hissed at Darcie, "You won't tell him what we're doing, will you? I don't trust him!"

Darcie waved off the objections and whispered back that she hadn't made up her mind yet. "But I still want more information about getting big bucks."

With drinks, handed around by Josh and Philip, in everyone's hands, their host settled on the floor, leaned back against the couch, crossed his legs, and muttered, "Where do I start? I guess I'll give you the short version tonight, and then I can fill in details later if you want."

Chapter Four

THE PAST AND THE FUTURE

Their host took a quick sip of his drink and began. "The Dome was built by an international group of people all feeling the world was corrupting them, their children, and a belief they called the Way. So they designed this dome. All who believed in a better way of life and would take an oath of allegiance were welcome. The total area would cover over three hundred square miles, and the cost would exceed several billion dollars." Philip forestalled Josh's question by saying, "I couldn't begin to show you how much that is because I have nothing for a measure. I believe it was an enormous amount of whatever you use to buy things."

Philip told them that no obstacle slowed this group down. "They had engineers and contractors who worked five years designing and redesigning. They had farmers and scientists create a self-supporting life system based on solar and battery power.

"Thousands of their followers bought acre after acre until they owned all the land around the empty post that would be enough to complete the design. When some of the early planners died before seeing the completion of their dream, they left their share of the dome to their families.

"After much discussion, one single door was kept available in case someone from the outside would seek sanctuary. Probably you four are the first ones through it since the Dome was completed. The news certainly never reported it if someone did. That's why I would really like you to consider doing at least one talk show before you leave."

Darcie evaded giving an answer once again. Instead, she asked him if he would tell them more about the Way. She had never heard of that term.

"As much as I can tell," he said, "it was a belief. You know, we have the belief here that you create your own destiny using hard work, and with a little good luck, your fortune is made. Their belief was in a prophet and some good teachings he had while he was alive. I can't find any of the teachings now. Your people took his writings into the Dome with them, and when they became illegal out here, the civil war destroyed all copies or people hid them so well they're lost forever. One of the main goals of the war was completely stamping out this belief and all his teachings. Like you, we tried to make the playing field level for everyone. So we passed rules and laws and didn't allow any standards that would allow comparisons. But without any reason to do well, we've ended up with mostly chaos and a lot of jobs not filled because they are beneath our talents. So maybe you can get me a copy of those lost teachings? Boy, would that set this land on its ear! They'd surely give me money for research then!"

Josh asked, "Darcie, does he mean the Bib? That's the only teachings I know about." He faced Philip. "She bragged about sneaking a peek. She can tell you."

Darcie glared at Josh, but she knew ignoring Philip's interest wasn't going to happen.

"Every home in the Dome has a Bib. It's a huge book and sits in the front room on a pedestal. When you turn twelve, you can open it and read as much or as little as you want each day for the rest of your life. When I was younger, Dad would read out of it every night. It was boring, and I yawned a lot. Then Dad became one of the leaders for our block and had lots of meetings and not much time for home, so now, mostly Mom just dusts it. I sneaked a peek when I was ten and everyone was shopping. It has a lot of sayings in it. The last part of the book has bunches of words written in red. It didn't mean much to me then, and when I could read it, I didn't want to. I don't know that many who are my age who have read it."

Philip was excited. "Can't you remember anything you read? Don't they teach it in your schools? Your people fought that one thing with the government. The schools wouldn't teach what this man said. We won that battle big time out here, and it was going to have a prominent place in your schools."

Darcie responded, "I don't know what a school is. We spend our days in learning centers. I don't know who this man is either. Who cares what his teachings were?"

She was getting angry, feeling swept along in a current and losing control of the situation and answering more questions than she was asking.

"I'm getting tired of all your questions! We appreciate your hospitality, but if you expect us doing a bunch of things for you in return, then I'd rather we leave now and take our chances on the streets. We're tired, and we have to leave early tomorrow. Our folks are expecting us back soon."

Philip lifted his hands in immediate surrender. "Okay, the questions can wait for now. You do not want to spend the night on our streets! However, can I offer some practical help? Tell me where you want to go, and I'll see if I can help get you there. Don't forget, I make my living taking people where they want to go. Then, since I've helped you, you can help me."

He was relaxed and smiling again.

Janna was huddled under a blanket she had found on the back of the couch, and Josh was having trouble keeping his eyes open. Juli and Darcie communicated with a long glance, and then Juli nodded.

Juli rocked back against the couch and clasped her hands around her legs. "We're looking for someone called the Eternal One. We have a problem in the Dome, and no one can figure out the answer. We kept hearing the grown-ups talking about him and his wisdom. We couldn't find much about him in our Dome books, but I think we've figured out that he lives somewhere in the mountains. So, we're going to the first mountain on our path."

Their host raised his eyebrows. "That's quite an undertaking. Did you kids leave the Dome based on that little bit of information? So you're just going to walk until you stumble across someone who

42

identifies himself as the Eternal One? Maybe you're looking for me and didn't know it.

"And how have you solved your problem of food, water, and shelter while you're searching? Those backpacks of yours don't seem to be stuffed. Do you realize that it'll be two more days before you reach the peak of even the closest mountain? And what if that one isn't the right one? There are hundreds of mountains, at different heights, for fifty miles from here."

Again, the two friends exchanged glances. Darcie sighed and answered, "It seemed like a good idea at the time. We had a camping guide to start with, but it got ruined. And so we didn't have much to go on. We brainstormed and tried to imagine every possible situation to plan for and packed as best we could. We have some food left, but we figured there would be places to rest and restaurants to get food from. But except for you, that hasn't happened.

"Now I don't know, but," she added quickly, "we are going on. It was hard planning for the unknown, so if you have any advice about how we can finish our mission, I'd like to hear it."

With obvious reluctance, Philip explained the terrain between the town and the mountain. He gave them a map showing them how to leave town fairly unnoticed and resume their trek to the mountain. With no roads in the mountain mapped, he hand-drew a trail they could follow that would get them to the summit within two or three days. Juli had pointed out, in their conversation, that the "seven-day rule" would happen during this trip, and they wanted to be as close to the Dome as possible. The entire day of rest on this seventh day would be easier for them if they could see the Dome from where they would be stopping.

Juli noted, "We could see the Dome for about three and one-half hours before the hills got tall enough to hide it. Although we can't travel more than four hours on the seventh day, we would at least be close to home. I truly hope we are not still on that mountain."

Philip Conner, fascinated with all the tidbits of information he was picking up, went to his cupboards. Although he didn't have much variety, he was able to pack enough food to help them for a few days. He assured them there was plenty of food available along the way and showed them pictures of berries growing and fruit ripe for this time of year. When he confirmed that fish was a staple of their diet, he explained they could find mountain streams where they would find plenty of fish and probably the berries and fruit as well.

Using a short wooden stick with a red tip that he plucked from a small box, he scraped the tip across a rough surface on the outside of the box, and fire erupted from the tip. The girls gasped and drew back.

He chuckled in amazement. "Use these matches to light the sticks you'll find on the trail, and you will keep warm at night. And the fire could be some protection in case you meet some hungry animal."

Darcie swallowed and asked, "How will that small light help?"

She touched her finger into the flame and quickly snatched it back. "Ouch!"

Philip shook out the match. "Are you for real? You don't know what a match and open fire are?"

"Fire?" Juli shook her head. "I've never heard of it. What's it used for?"

Philip chuckled, "For heat and cooking! Open flame isn't the only way we do these things, but it's often used. And on the trail, it's about all you'll use. How in the world could you have lost the use of fire?"

Juli shrugged. "We push a button or turn a dial. I never went on any of the tours of our power plants, but I'm sure they don't use fire. Usually, our outdoors is the same temperature as our indoors, so we're comfortable either place without doing anything special."

Showing them a hole in his wall that he called a fireplace, Philip demonstrated the proper way to build a fire that would burn for hours with just minor maintenance. Josh, who had been struggling with sleep, watched in rapt attention.

Philip remarked that they, at least, had appropriate clothing for their long hike. Darcie and Juli exchanged smiles. Juli explained, "When we go to maintenance camp for a month, one of the places we have to serve is in the catacombs. They are a little cooler than the surface, so they equip us with these denim outfits that are like our normal play clothes but have zippered sleeves and legs. When we're down under, we zip the sleeves and legs on. Then, above ground, we just have to unzip them, and we have shorts and short-sleeved shirts. The shoes, issued for the ability to walk around on sometimes slick routes where the spring might drip in, are standard gear. We try hard to keep it all dry underground, but that's one of the missions of the summer group. We're constantly patching the seeps and repacking some of the supplies kept in there. We also maintain the burial plots. Since we had told our folks that's where we'd be the next few weeks, we got the full complement, including some nice warm jackets. We packed all we could but had to leave our good clothes behind and will need to wash the clothes we packed at some point or wear them dirty."

Phillip nodded and explained that when they found a stream near to where they would spend the night, they should rinse their clothes and dry them over their fire. He made a special point of explaining the need to keep their socks dry and as clean as possible to prevent blisters.

The clock ticked closer to nine, Philip stretched and rose. "Let me go to the kitchen, and I'll work on some camping instructions for you to use. It's important when you make camp for the night to do it right. Although I normally won't keep anyone out on the trail after dark, there are tips I've learned when I do my gold mining that will come in handy for you. You guys should start thinking about getting some rest."

Darcie felt she should see if he knew something that would overcome the darkness lurking just outside the windows.

"Mr. Conner, there has never been a night of my life when our outdoors was as dark as this one. Our streetlights make it almost as light as daytime. There is a rule about not allowing the darkness because of the evil there. I am anxious that we meet no evil on our trip. Is there a way we can carry light with us? How do you protect yourself against the evil?"

Philip Conner disappeared into the kitchen and returned with a cylindrical object in his hand. "We call these flashlights. I've got several, and I'll put them with the rest of the stuff I want you to borrow.

Maybe you should consider taking me along on this adventure as a kind of guide?"

Darcie, taken aback, stuttered, "Oh, oh! No, really, no, that won't be necessary. Just help us all you can now, and we'll let you get back to your life. We really couldn't ask you to come, and I know you have your job to do. And we appreciate all you've done, but this is our problem. But thanks! Uh, it's after nine. Could we sleep now?" Darcie ground to a stop.

Disappointment deepened the lines on his face, making Philip look older and less kindly.

"Yeah, sure, kids. Call it a night. I'll get your supplies together, along with the instructions on how to use them. On this map I'm making, I'll mark the cave where I do most of my mining. I keep supplies there all the time, and since it's closer to your home than town, why don't you just leave my stuff there? I'll be as quiet as I can in the kitchen. Then I'll just run upstairs and stay with a friend of mine and let you guys have the bed."

The girls looked around for the bed until he started taking cushions off the couch. He tugged at a hanging tag and pulled; the insides of the couch came spilling out onto the floor. Thin legs unfolded, and the result became a bed. The girls giggled.

Philip returned to the kitchen, leaving them to get ready for whatever rest they would find. Darcie experimented with the flashlight. She had Juli turn off the lights and checked the amount of the room the flashlight illuminated.

"I'm sure glad I asked. I feel much better having a few of these along."

Juli shook her head. "You know, he didn't say they would ward off evil. In fact, he seemed to ignore that question entirely. I wish I had paid more attention during our weekly teachings. My parents were always discussing it. Somehow, I feel like they would have some good advice about all this. Don't know if we could even recognize evil if we saw it."

"Don't worry!" Darcie hugged her. "I just know we'll be okay. Let's get some sleep. Things will look better in the morning."

Although Darcie's body ached with fatigue, the strange surroundings and the noises coming from the kitchen didn't allow her to fall into sleep quickly. She longed for a deep refreshing sleep, but instead, she could hear the tossing and turning of the twins sleeping on the hard floor with just a few couch cushions under them and a thin blanket on top. Juli was equally restless and could be heard muttering in her sleep. So even though the night seemed endless, morning came long before the weary travelers were ready.

Black faded gradually into gray, and birds began to tune their voices. Finally, the sunlight reached in and touched Janna's eyelids, and she rolled over on her back. She poked her brother and grabbed her sister's toe hanging off the bed above her eyes.

Everyone was sore and irritable, and unkind words were spoken as the small bathroom was impatiently waited for.

Later, in the kitchen, they found the supplies Philip had donated. On top of one of the piles was a note. Philip apologized that he couldn't say goodbye. His friend was having a crisis and needed his support. So he had quietly left early in the morning, leaving the note and the list of tips he had prepared that should help them reach their destination. The note finished with "Hope you can stop back sometime soon, and maybe you could do that interview. Good luck!"

The reaction to the note varied. Darcie was both pleased and regretful. She had almost decided she would allow him to take some of the burden and sign on as their guide. Yet she struggled with giving away any of the leadership.

Janna was only concerned for her empty stomach because she had expected a hot breakfast.

Josh felt disappointed that he hadn't been able to at least say goodbye to his new friend.

Juli was thoughtfully silent.

Chapter Five

ON THE MOUNTAIN

After dividing the new equipment and food among the backpacks, Juli served the cold cereal and toasted the bread she found on the counter. Sweeping the final crumbs off the counter and into the garbage, she led them quietly out of the apartment.

Their quest resumed as Josh took a path allowing them to find a careful way out of town using walkways between the buildings and avoiding any populated area.

Darcie, turning back from time to time to glance over her shoulder, finally gave the all-clear signal. But she didn't allow any talking until they reached some of the taller shrubs and walked over the crest of the closest hill. Happily, she saw the town swallowed up from their sight.

Josh set a pace that ate up the miles yet was not tiring.

Juli, always ready with an encouraging word, remarked, "This is a much better day than yesterday. I don't seem to be as tired as quickly."

Janna complained, "Maybe it's good for you, but I'm starting to get another blister. Who has the Band-Aids?"

Darcie called a halt and fished the pads out of her backpack. She handed around some fruit and made sure everyone took some sips of water. "I feel better about the new provisions. It's nice knowing I don't have to worry about rationing the food and water. Mr. Conner promised we'd find plenty.

"Come on, Janna. Get your shoes back on. You're doing better today too. You've only made us stop this one time, and yesterday it seemed like it was every five minutes you had something to complain about."

Josh, who carried the hand-drawn map Philip had made, announced he was going ahead to the top of the next hill to make sure they were on the right path.

The girls giggled as he strode off. Janna whispered, "Can you wear out a compass? We'd better make sure he gives it back to Mr. Conner."

Juli said as she drew in a breath of the sweet, tranquil air, "Oh, let him have his fun. Besides, he does seem to know what he's doing. It's too nice a day to pick on anyone."

Darcie moved down the path, noting how increasingly hilly the terrain was, and pointed out how large stones seemed to be randomly placed. She mused, "It's like a couple of giants were having a rock-throwing contest. It's pretty bleak out here. Down close to that town, the pastures were smooth and green. Here the grass is scraggly and just grows in clumps. Evergreens or white birch are about the only trees in sight."

The first sight of the sun touching the top of the hill in front of the path he was climbing was when Josh was able to point to the entrance to the small canyon.

"It's here just as Mr. Conner told me. Here's where he said to spend our first night. See on the map, here's the small stream. He said to camp beside it. I can catch some fish for supper, and you guys can pick some of those berries over there. With the rice we've packed, it'll taste good."

Darcie motioned them to the clearing just beside the rushing stream. White birch trees stood as sentinels, and lush green grass rose knee-high. Philip had instructed them how they could tramp down a circle of that grass and make their camp on top.

Juli gazed at the darkening sky. She pulled the attention of the rest when she said, "Look at that anvil-shaped cloud and all the dark ones behind it. There was only one day in the Center where we discussed clouds, but I was intrigued. They were so beautiful, and we aren't able to see them in the Dome. Now, if I remember rightly, that is a storm cloud. I don't think we're going to enjoy tonight."

Darcie and Juli exchanged glances. Josh spoke up, "Want me go up the stream a ways and see if I can find more shelter than this? I've got the compass, and I won't go far. Conner said to stay away from trees if it's stormy."

With obvious reluctance, Darcie nodded, and Josh whooped. He dropped his backpack and, with long strides, moved toward the stream's bank. The stony shore gave him good footing, and within minutes, he was at the bend of the river that would take him from sight.

The girls stood silently with just the sound of rushing water to fill the void.

They seemed incomplete now, yet they still had camp to set up.

Bending over their backpacks on the ground and starting to remove their gear, Juli's head snapped up at a yell from Josh. Standing at the bed of the stream, he was frantically waving.

Darcie grabbed the pack Joshua had tossed to the ground and, as fast as the bags banging Darcie's legs would allow, she ran toward her friend.

As she got closer, she saw a grin on his face. He yelled, "You'll never guess what I found! It's like it was put here just for us."

Panting slightly, the girls closed the gap to where Josh stood poised to walk around the bend again. They followed and stopped dead in their tracks.

Acting as a tour guide, Josh flung out his arm, deepened his voice, and presented, "Nested beside the flowing stream, water-wheel turning, stands an old abandoned mill. Made of stone blocks, it stands two stories high, and surprisingly enough, still has several windows intact. The walls are standing strong, with a shade tree as a rigid guard before the gaping hole that was the door. Here, miladies, is our room for the night."

Darcie, breathing a quiet sigh of relief, laughed at Josh's theatrics. "Thank you, Mr. Tour Guide."

With an eye to the sky, she quickly took charge. "We'll collect all the wood we can find, and I mean every scrap. There's a chimney, so let's hope there's a hole like Mr. Conner has in his house. We'll be warm and dry. Get enough to make sure we don't run out in the middle of the night."

She assigned Joshua the task of laying out the sleeping bags. She instructed, "Make sure you clean this floor up first. I don't want anything in my bag except me. Then, go fish."

Janna went to the stream, filled their canteens, and brought in cooking water.

Juli got the borrowed pans out, lit a match to the kindling, and placed the pot with the water for the rice on the blackened grill in the fireplace. Josh had made short work on their bedroom and quickly moved to the task he had been anticipating.

His fishing went well, and soon Juli was cleaning and cutting up the fish he had proudly dropped at her side.

Darcie, meanwhile, returning from her search for sticks, enlisted the help of the twins to drag in more branches while supper was cooking. And then she, using the unfamiliar hatchet, broke up the larger sticks and piled them near the fire hole.

After supper and cleanup, she took the map from Josh and studied it. "Are you sure you can find the cave Mr. Conner marked? I would rather leave everything there and not go back to his home. He was a nice guy and everything, but he made me feel weird. I did like his idea about big bucks though. Too bad that didn't work out."

Juli, sitting with her back against the cold stone wall, voiced her thoughts. "I don't think I liked him from the first. You're right. He seemed nice enough, but something didn't feel right. I vote we find that cave rather than go back too."

Josh hurled an acorn he found on the floor out the open doorway. "What's wrong with you two anyhow? I don't know where you get your ideas sometimes. All this guy did was to let us borrow all this equipment and didn't charge us and trusts we'll return it, and you make him sound like he's a germ. I liked him. And when I get on my own, I'm coming back for a visit."

His twin, who had crawled into her sleeping bag right after cleanup, roused herself, complaining, "Can't you guys pipe down? Who cares about some creepy old man? And I'll bet you, Josh, that you won't come back here. You'll forget all about him. 'Sides, I agree with the girls. There's something strange about him. You're dumb and never look farther than your nose. Now shut up, and let's get some sleep!"

Darcie arose and stretched. "I agree. I'm for bed. Stay awake during your watches, and don't let the fire go out. That storm seems to be still hanging out there. Good night."

A scant hour later, Juli tossed another stick on the glowing coals of their fire and returned to her perch beside the empty doorway. Just as she sank onto her wadded-up sleeping bag, a jagged streak of light flashed to the ground closely followed by a mighty boom. She gasped and turned to the others, who were no longer asleep.

"Did you see that?" she questioned.

"I didn't see anything, but that was a noisy alarm clock. What's going on?" queried Darcie.

The night sky outside again lit up with three spikes of lighting flashing down to the ground. Close behind the light, a sonic boom chased the light in a futile attempt to catch it. In the deadly quiet that followed, the wind jumped into the branches of the tree before them and began tossing the limbs as if to tear them from their trunk. Rain splattered the hard, rocky ground in drops that quickly turned into a hard downpour.

"I think we're getting the storm those clouds threatened. We should be okay in here. I don't see any water coming in from the ceiling. Wow! It's one thing to sit in a classroom learning the meaning of the word *storm* but quite another to see the wind, rain, thunder, and lightning that is a storm firsthand. This is wild!" Josh had a grin from ear to ear.

Juli drew back away from the doorway as a gust of wind tossed some rain at her. She laughed. "Well, good luck getting any sleep while this is going on."

But even this magnificent show in the sky couldn't keep the tired trio from soon drifting back into the dark calm of sleep.

Juli continued her watch. The storm didn't frighten her. Instead, she seemed to be in awe of what she saw and heard.

She silently watched until the storm passed.

Sunlight slanted through the dust beams at the open door and splashed on Janna's face, sounding the alarm of another day.

Her watch finished, Janna roused the others. Again, the morning started with little conversation. They divided some trail mix for their breakfast, packed their gear, and cleaned up the mill room in companionable silence.

Shortly after resuming the trail, it soon became clear that now all the paths moved uphill. Darcie noticed that her legs became tired quickly, and she called for rest stops more frequently where she massaged her cramped calves.

Janna, who could talk when no one else had anything to say, found little energy to speak but still managed to complain as the air grew thinner and the ascent steeper.

Juli's feet slipped on the small pebbles on the trail. Her hand shot out and stopped her fall, yet she managed to skin her right knee.

She decided that this would probably be their most uncomfortable night they would have to endure since leaving the Dome. When they could finally see the summit ahead, she was the first to vote to stop where they were for the night rather than risk getting to the top in the dark.

Josh found another small clearing under a canopy of spruce trees. He made sure they had a view of the white-capped mountain for their supper-time pleasure, trusting that this was their final destination. The mountain he was climbing seemed high enough. He had given his share of speculation about what lay on the now-close white, pure, and bright peak.

He did know that the night time air was colder, colder than anything he had ever experienced. Josh said, "The Dome doesn't have anything to complain about until it gets this cold in there."

Darcie grumbled under her breath as the search for firewood became a challenge with fewer trees surrounding the path, and the kind of tree that was the choice of this landscape didn't obligingly drop their old branches waiting for the fire.

Josh, forced back down the mountain in search for water, had to lug the filled canteens back up the steep slope. Juli fought with the fire as the thin air made it burn unevenly.

Darcie set up the tents, and Janna used the hatchet to cut off low-hanging green boughs. Juli coughed in the smoky fire but commented on how aromatic it made the air.

Even while doing the chores, Darcie would find herself looking up at the top of the mountain, knowing that tomorrow could be the climax of the trip.

Wondering if her quest would end in rocks and a nice view and if he was there, what would the Eternal One look like? And what would she have to decide if he wasn't there? Should they try another mountain, still further away? Should they return to the Dome and never discuss this trip? She could have them back in time to maintain the lie that they were doing maintenance.

She knew from the upward glances of her fellow travelers that these thoughts and more tumbled through their minds as well. They were probably as restless and apprehensive as she was.

Janna, who had the first watch, reached into the tent, and shook Juli's shoulder. "Can you come and keep me company?"

Startled and dazed, Juli crawled out of the tent and stood beside her younger sister.

"Listen!" Janna placed her finger on her lips. "Hear that moaning sound, and watch the trees below us. Their branches are swaying back and forth, but I don't feel any wind. What is it?"

Juli shook her head slowly. "Hon, I don't know. This is a strange place to live, yet it feels like home. There sure is a lot of beauty that we are missing living in the Dome. The wind here seems to play games and be where you least expect it. There have been times it even seems to want to speak to me."

She glanced at her watch. "It feels like I just closed my eyes, but I see it's almost time for me to take over. Why don't you go to bed now?"

Janna gratefully went into the tent, and Juli sat quietly by the smoking fire. She leaned forward and gazed down the mountain side. Again, although alone in a strange place with just her own thoughts for company, she felt calm and peaceful. The top of this mountain held no danger for her.

Chapter Six

THE ENCOUNTER

As the dawn light touched the sky and pink streaked the gray, Juli bestirred herself. Again, she had spent most of the night in silent contemplation, allowing the others to sleep. Now she woke them, and the day started slowly and stiffly.

Josh, as he wolfed his powdered eggs, addressed his older sister, "Hey, Sis! You all right? You're so quiet."

The smile that touched Juli's lips reflected the peace found in her eyes. She said, "I'm just fine. The closer we get to the top, the better I feel. Let's hurry and get up there. I just feel there's something wonderful waiting for us."

Josh noted that breaking camp didn't take long any more. He hoisted the pack to Janna's back and helped adjust the straps. He turned his face to the sun that was just peeking over the edge of the world. He moved them single file up the trail.

Although the summit had appeared to be only about another hour's worth of trekking, when the morning wore on and they seemed no closer to their goal, Josh referred to his map again and again, finally putting it away.

"I'm not sure I understand what's going on," he complained. "According to the map, we're on the right path to reach the top. We can see it from here, and yet the path must twist and turn so much that we're walking miles and still aren't there. Maybe we should just go straight up and work ourselves around the boulders and trees and get off this no-end path."

Janna leaned against an enormous stone and wiped her brow. "I don't care what we do, but let's get to the top soon. This is wearing me out. It's so hard to breathe, and that wind sure is cold."

So after another brief rest, Joshua pulled them off the beaten path they had been following, and he aimed them towards a tree that hung over the edge of the summit of the mountain they traveled.

The going was treacherous, and Josh quickly devised a plan where he would take the point and wrap a rope around a close tree and the girls could use it to pull themselves up to the next stage of the trail. This sped up the process, although Josh was always waiting impatiently for the rope so he could climb the next leg. He rested while the girls climbed; they rested while he climbed to the next tie-off point.

Shortly before noon, Joshua touched the overhanging tree and laughed. He quickly made a knot and tossed the coil down. One by one, he watched the girls climb hand over hand. Josh pulled Darcie up the last foot of rope and turned to join them on the ledge, seeing a breathtaking backdrop of blue-tinted mountains lying in front of this peak they stood on.

Looking down, Juli saw the countryside spread out around them. She pointed to a blue lake as it sparkled in the sun.

"I couldn't begin to describe this scene to anyone. It's so beautiful that words couldn't paint a good-enough picture. They would have to see this contrast of the blue of the cloudless sky, the deeper huckleberry of the lake, and everywhere below the various shades of green from trees and grass spotted with the vivid hues of the flowers. Man, I sound like our museum guide!" Juli laughed.

Darcie turned in a circle. "Hello," she whispered, "is anyone here?"

Janna humphed. "Shouldn't you talk a little louder?"

"Probably," retorted Darcie, "but it doesn't seem right. You know?"

No one stood to greet her. As she glanced around the barren rock, she realized that, in fact, there was no place for anyone to hide from them, if that was the intent. The ledge she stood on, the highest point of this mountain, was empty. Except for the one tree where Josh had tied their rope, there was no grass and no flowers—just a series of jagged rocks sticking up between her and the sky and rocky ledges that climbed down away from her perch.

"Oh, this is just great," groused Darcie. "All this time and work, and there isn't anyone here. I suppose this means we have to try somewhere else."

She tossed her backpack away from her and sank down on a protruding flat rock.

She watched the siblings also find a place to sit and discard the weight on their backs.

Juli, unwilling to be the first to voice the fear of a wasted trip, stretched out on her hard bed. She encouraged the others by saying, "Let's grab a quick nap. Suddenly, I'm so tired I can't keep my eyes open. We'll have a meeting before lunch and decide our next step."

Her eyes closed as she laid her head down.

Juli's dream started with a bolt of jagged lightning followed by the rumbling of thunder. The earth shook and rolled her off her ledge, knocking her to her knees.

A man with a bright light at his back walked toward her. Although she couldn't see his features or see his mouth move, a voice filled the air and said, "I am the One you seek. I would have answered you wherever you called My name, even in the Dome. But your people have lost that knowledge, so I allowed your trip."

Immeasurable joy filled Juli as she looked upon the spot she thought was His face. Although the light was extremely bright, it didn't hurt her eyes. She leaned forward, hands together and listened to His sweet voice. In amazement, she heard her instructions regarding the answer they sought. Suddenly, things were clear and precise. Told of tools and helps He would furnish, she knew, without a doubt, that she was in the presence of the Eternal One.

With a start, Juli was awake and again on her rock bed. The others around her were sitting up and looking at her and one another.

She wondered if her face had the same peaceful yet astonished look that she saw on her friends.

Josh broke into excited speech, "I've just had the strangest but greatest dream. I know the reason we're here."

Darcie, Juli, and Janna spoke over each other.

"Me too."

"Wait until you hear mine."

"It was too cool!"

Darcie waved her hands. "Wait, wait! Let's do this one at a time. I'm assuming we all had a dream?" She paused and looked around at the nods. "Wow, okay. Then let's compare notes. Wow! This is awesome. Josh, we'll let you go first since you're the only guy."

So he told of his encounter with the Man in the Light. The Man called him by name and told Josh that he would teach the people in the Dome the things they had forgotten.

Janna hugged herself. "Wow! I've never felt like I did while He was talking to me. I feel like I just had a bath on my insides. I feel different!"

Josh could only whisper once again, "He called me by my name!"

Juli, with tears of joy running a track down her dusty cheeks, said, "It was the most special thing that has ever happened to me. He told me that there would be tools for me to find and use. He told me I had a special gift and I was to use it for the good of everyone. It was like being in a field full of flowers and all I had to do was enjoy them."

Darcie turned toward the western sky and pointed at the pink streaks. "We have about four or five hours of sunlight left. Do we stay here or start back down and go until its dark?"

Josh looked around the barren top and answered, "There is no firewood here, and I see no way to put up the tents. I'd like to start down and see how far we get. Using the ropes again to go down, it shouldn't take us long to get back to where we spent last night."

"Okay," Darcie agreed. "Then let's grab a bite to eat and get cracking."

Soon after, Josh dropped the rope down the side and moved to let his twin pass. Reversing the order going down, he would have to untie the rope and climb down behind the girls without the benefit of any help. Yet he seemed taller in stature, and this challenge didn't daunt him.

As he reached the last tree where the girls waited for him, he knew they were only a few hours away from their last camping spot.

He guided them around a bend where he saw, lined up along the path, a helmet, a sword, a breastplate, and a shield.

Josh ran ahead, his words floating over his shoulder. "These are the tools He promised. I wonder which one is mine!"

Darcie yelled, "Come on," and sprinted after him.

Janna hopped up and down. "Are there any names on them? What funny things He left us. Come on, Josh, give me something!"

Darcie and Juli had been examining the pieces closely. Juli picked up the breastplate and held it against her chest.

"Nope, it'd be a tight fit for me. Come here, Janna. I think this is yours."

"Oh, you're kidding!" Janna pushed at Juli's hands. "I wanted the helmet. Let me try the helmet on or maybe the sword. I don't wanna wear that heavy thing."

But the helmet was too big and fell down over her eyes, and the sword was so heavy she couldn't carry it. The breastplate, however, buckled around her as if it was part of her skin. Made of lightweight leather, it molded itself to her body and buckled with two straps joined in the front.

The helmet was also made of leather but was more padded than the breastplate. It settled on Josh's head firmly.

Josh picked up the short sword lying on the grass. He hefted it and guessed it weighed about five pounds. He laid the blade along his arm and announced the shaft was about fifteen inches long. Passed around, everyone exclaimed how heavy the metal piece felt until it came to Darcie's turn. She handled it as if it was only a couple of ounces.

That left the leather-covered shield. It was round in shape with a twenty-inch radius. The leather strap fit Juli's arm without a single adjustment.

Now suited with the tools given them, Juli, with authority, admonished the rest, "Remember, we must stay together, and don't let go of this stuff until we're home."

Janna sulkily said, "What about sleeping and eating and other things? What if it gets heavy or makes me itch? Can't I take it off and let one of you carry it for a while?"

Josh spoke sharply, "Look, we better do what He says! Don't you still feel the power? Aren't you just a little afraid of Him? Don't you believe He knows what He's doing?"

"Well, 'course I do, silly! Still, I don't think He's gonna care all that much if you carried it for just a mile or so." She hastened on as Josh's frown deepened, "But if it means that much to you, then I'll wear it."

As she turned and trudged down the path, Juli heard her mutter, "I'd still rather have the helmet."

Darcie brandished her sword. "Let's go. I feel like I could slay lions and conquer worlds. Let's get back home and give them the answer. Let's tell them about this trip and everything He told us. Let's make a difference!"

She turned down the path. She felt light, almost floating down this descent. As she headed for their camp last night, she chattered about how she felt, about what was on the path ahead of them tomorrow, and about what the answer to the Dome's problem would be. She looked around at the peculiar tools they had received and talked with Juli about the gifts they received.

Time passed quickly; and Josh, with his map and compass, kept them on the path.

Janna was the only one who reminded them they hadn't had much lunch; although, as soon as she mentioned it, everyone was suddenly starving.

Even with suppertime not far off, Darcie called a halt and decided to hand out some trail mix. She had discovered the trick of thrusting her sword into her belt where her hand brushed it, comforting with almost every movement.

She thought of how Josh's helmet, as he walked ahead, had seemed like a banner that she could see and feel confident about that, with his compass, they were on the right path.

Juli marveled aloud that the shield didn't seem any heavier than when she had first picked it up. The straps hadn't chafed her arm. They agreed it had been very useful in pushing back the brambles that seemed intent on hindering their path.

Even Janna admitted, when questioned, that the breastplate caused her no discomfort. However, her face didn't reflect the same contentment found with the others.

Joshua led them down the mountain all that afternoon. At one point, they stopped beside a waterfall crashing down the mountainside. Spray drifted in the air as they filled their canteens in a side pool. Green grass abounded, and early fall flowers painted the scene with splashy colors.

As the valley drew near, they became quieter. Soon they could see below the path that wandered across the badlands—the path they had to walk. Josh turned and asked, "Should we spend the night here on the mountain or keep going until we reach the valley?"

Juli and Janna voted for staying on the mountain as they had planned, but now Darcie urged them on. "Remember, He told us to go quickly."

Juli pointed out that He had also said that they must stay together. "It'll be dark in less than an hour, and the valley isn't all that close. Then we'd still need time for setting up camp. No, let's just find our spot from last night, spend this night on the mountain, and face the valley tomorrow. We also have to wait for the answer. It must be on this path somewhere, like our tools."

The entire day had been with no friction in the group, but now Darcie set her lips. "Look, I really think we should go on. Sharing with the others what we've seen and giving them the answer is something that's important. Wasting time is wrong. Sitting here and going about our normal business doesn't seem right."

She held out her hand toward Josh. "Don't you feel the same? After all, He chose you as the spokesman. I'd think you couldn't wait."

A sudden gust of wind sprang up, and bits of wind-driven sand stung their faces and arms. As abruptly as it started, it was calm again.

Juli, who was on the brink of yielding to Darcie's passion, paused. The others glanced at each other, and Josh asked, "What was that all about?"

Juli blinked her eyes and focused on the faces around her. "I don't know, but it reminds me that we're to stay together because there are things out here we don't understand."

Her brother and sister nodded in agreement. Janna said, "Yes, let's just camp like we planned and get an early start tomorrow."

Darcie waved off the discussion. "Well, I'm not staying. I'm still going ahead tonight. I have the words He told me on the mountain, and when I find the answer on the path, I won't need your help in telling my dad. I think you three are wrong in staying on this mountain tonight. I'm just sure He would want us continuing on, even if we are a little tired and it's getting dark. Don't forget the seven-day rule is coming soon. And, Juli, you really disappoint me. I thought you would come with me, like always."

But Juli stood firm. "This time I'm not letting you talk me into anything." Sadly, she added, "I feel you're wrong. If you go alone, something could happen, and no one would know. I love you and care…"

"I love you too," broke in Darcie, "and I wish you'd go with me. We always do everything together."

"I'm honestly sorry, but I'm hearing something that's even stronger than my friendship with you. I'm doing what I feel is right. I can't follow after you on this."

She started crying quietly, and Darcie hurriedly picked up her pack. "Please don't cry! I'll tell your parents that you're coming behind me."

With quick hugs given, Darcie stopped and waved once before the trail bent and swallowed her up.

It was as if all sound ceased when Darcie lost sight of her friends. Silence pressed in on her ears and was almost painful. The first taste of uneasiness touched her heart.

Her hand automatically gripped the sword in her belt. She mentally and physically flung back her shoulders, puckered her lips, and began whistling.

The rocks around muted her brave noise, and the loneliness seemed more solid than the stone wall beside her. The path was uneven and wound between the rock wall and a sheer drop-off. The gentle breeze she had felt since the encounter with the Eternal One was her only company.

Darkness dropped on her like someone had thrown a blanket over her head, and she stopped and dug out her flashlight. She shone the beam down the path in a vain attempt to see what lay ahead, so she missed the rock that was right under her feet, the rock that spun out as she stepped on it. Suddenly, she couldn't find her balance. Arms flailing the air, feet slipping on the pebbles, Darcie fell off the path, landed on her back, and began sliding down the mountain.

So full of terror that she couldn't even scream, Darcie twisted around, and her hands and feet scrabbled for any kind of hold that would slow her descent. Her heart was pounding, and her lungs felt starved for air.

A slow-motion slide of the rocks around her turned into a powerless slide. Small avalanches started as her propelled body dislodged stones and rocks. They showered down on her head. She dug her fingers into the hard ground she was slipping down only to have her nails break as they were rejected by the stone. Trying to use her hands as brakes only resulted in them becoming scrapped and cut.

Without being aware of a conscious thought, she twisted her body enough so she could slide the short sword out. In a swift, desperate stroke, she thrust it into the unforgiving mountain whose mouth seemed to open and suck it in. Grasping the shaft with both hands, her slide jerked to a stop. A few rocks still trickled down, bouncing off her head and smacking down on her bleeding, gripping hands, but she held on, lying with her face in the dust that billowed up around her prone body.

When she started hearing, seeing, and thinking again, she became aware that she had been uttering repeatedly "Thank you! Thank you!" But who was she thanking?

Curiosity made her peer over her shoulder. Only darkness loomed below her. There was no bottom in sight and not even a ledge where she could set her feet until daylight. Suddenly, finding a place to rest was the most important thing to do.

Even now, her fingers were growing numb, and the strain on her arm sockets made the sweat stand out on her forehead. She could not remain here! She knew she didn't have the strength to crawl up this mountain, and letting go and continuing her slide into the unknown was definitely not an option.

She dug her toes into the dirt and pushed her body up, attempting to relieve some of the pressure on her arms. There was no mountain bigger, no night darker, and never had she felt more helpless and alone.

The gentle breeze dried her tears and brought her a sound—a faint sound—of someone whistling.

At first, attempting a cry made her cough as dust filtered into her nose. The next try sent a "Help!" vibrating off the cold rock walls. Once started, her screams were almost nonstop until her throat began hurting. Then she could hear a calm, quiet voice above her declaring, "You're all right now."

The blurred face of a stranger stared down at her. Even from the distance, her drawn gaze saw only His gentle smile and the serene look on His face.

"I'm coming down to get you. Just hang on."

"Please hurry. My fingers are cramping, and I don't think I can hold on much longer."

She could only hear faint noises for the next few minutes. Then a rope snaked down beside her, followed shortly by the legs of the man. The cramps in her fingers were intolerable, and at the precise moment that her numb fingers slipped off the handle, His arm encircled her waist and He hugged her against His chest.

She snuggled inside His arm, feeling secure and safe—the scratch of His clothes comforting her. He held her tight for a time then said, "Pull your sword out, and put it in your belt. Let's climb up now."

She leaned into His chest and clasped her arms around His neck as He wrapped His hands around the rope and slowly walked back up the mountain with the ease of long practice.

Back on the path, her knees wouldn't support her weight as the reaction to her near miss turned her muscles to jelly. He lowered her onto the dirt. She watched her savior coil the rope and carry it over near the large rock He had used for an anchor.

Rope in hand, He walked around the other side to untie the knot.

Darcie waited for His return, knowing that she owed Him her life and wondering what she could say that would show even a particle of the gratitude she felt. She waited and waited.

Finally, she shakily stood up and walked in the direction of the large anchoring rock. She walked around the large stone that was now without a rope. She peered around in the dark but saw no one moving. She called, "Mister?"

An owl hooted in answer.

She was alone, yet she didn't feel alone. She could still feel the strength of His arms and the tenderness as He carried her. She knew she would never forget this man, and she knew He was responsible for this second chance at life she now had. She hoped she would see Him again and He would smile as she would tell of the things she had done because of the extra time He had given her.

The moon came out from behind the clouds and became a lamp for her feet as she moved back up the path where her friends camped. Her pack was still on her back, but the flashlight was gone. So the moonlight on the path was all she had to find her way, but it seemed to be more than enough. She hugged the wall side of the path and moved back up the trail to be with the ones who cared and loved her.

Chapter Seven

DROPPING THE GUARD

Darcie's friends were sitting around a welcoming fire as she entered the clearing. Janna spotted Darcie first and cried out her name. Everyone gathered around her, and they all talked at once. They drew Darcie over so she could feel the warmth of the campfire, and Juli laughingly said, "I hope you're hungry. I automatically made enough for you too."

As Darcie ate, she talked, and the listeners' eyes grew big and round. The audience applauded the happy ending.

Josh asked, "You mean, you couldn't even tell Him thank you?"

Darcie replied, "Well, I mean, I did say that as soon as He was close enough to hear, but it didn't seem enough. He risked His life too, but I wouldn't have the slightest idea what to say. So at least now I won't feel regret over the words not said and the few words that were. You know?"

Juli mused, "Was this man sent by the Eternal One?"

Darcie didn't have the answer to that. She just knew she was safe.

It took a little longer for the camp to settle down that night; and as Darcie drifted off, she again resolved she would lead her life in a way that would please the one who had saved her and put her feet on the right path. She felt warm and comfortable.

Sometime during that night, Janna awoke with the sure knowledge that she must avail herself of the outside restroom. She rolled over, telling herself she could ignore the unwanted pressure; but the leather breastplate she wore pushed into her side.

Angry now, she sat up and threw back her blanket, muttering, "Stupid old breastplate anyhow! I still don't see why I can't take it off for just a little while. I'd probably still be asleep if it wasn't for that stupid thing."

She stumbled down the path, tugging and pulling on the breastplate. As she neared the area Josh had prepared for their use, she stopped and peered around.

"No one will ever know, and besides, it won't make any difference," she muttered to herself.

Her breastplate fell to the ground. "I'll put it back on before anyone wakes up."

A few minutes later, she started back up the trail with her gift dangling from her fingertips. Suddenly, she was aware of a sharp sting in her chest. Before she could cry out or even think, she felt herself falling facedown in the dirt.

Janna's next sensation was of motion, but she wasn't doing the moving. Rather, it was her body moving. She lifted her spinning head and discovered she was lying across the back of a burro with her hands tied against the stirrups.

She opened her mouth to scream when a rough hand clasped her jaw and forced her teeth down on her tongue.

"Don't make a sound or I'll put you out again."

Through her pain, Janna recognized the voice. She blinked the tears from her eyes and stared. She was right. It was Philip Conner.

He sneered at her as he ripped off a piece of tape from his roll and smacked it on her lips. She lowered her head and concentrated on not getting sick from the pain of the saddle digging into her stomach as the burro's gait lurched her from side to side and her head flopped around unbidden.

She decided she must have slept or passed out because she became alert to her surroundings again only when the rough ride stopped. Philip Conner walked into her view, and she tried to lift her head enough to glare at him. He ignored her look, cutting the straps holding her wrists, and walked to the other side of the burro. He grabbed her belt and slid her off the saddle until her feet touched the ground.

Janna immediately reached up with her now-freed hands, tearing off the strip of tape, and screamed. Her captor shook his head in amusement. "Go ahead. There's no one who'll hear for miles."

She spun away to run from him, but he quickly reached out and grabbed her wrist, pinching her skin in his grip.

"Now don't! Don't force me to keep you tied. Look around. You don't even know where you are. You certainly don't know where your friends are. You have no food or water. Just sit down, and I'll explain everything."

But Janna hated even having her friends tell her what to do, so this man, who had befriended them and had now betrayed them, was certainly not going to dictate terms to her. So she struggled in his grip and pushed against his chest, trying to break free. Irrationally, she wasn't concerned about where she was or how far away her friends were. She only knew this was not where she wanted to be.

Philip took a firmer grip and dragged her back to the side of the donkey where the rope from the saddle lay on the ground. He pulled her over to a nearby tree and threw her on the ground. He tied first her wrists and then clinched the end of the rope around her feet. He looped the extra length around the small trunk and pulled the knot tight.

She sat, indignant and silent, against the scratchy bark of the tree and glared at him while she watched him build a fire and make breakfast. He talked to her as he worked, and she felt he was trying to justify his actions. "I have this all planned out. I need you kids as evidence. Getting my paper published will make me rich and famous. Now, if you remember right, I did ask nicely and even offered payment for an exclusive interview. I really thought I had Darcie convinced, but then Juli turned her against me.

"So I knew I wouldn't be able to take the direct approach, but my dad taught me there was more than one way to skin a cat. I was real glad I could talk Darcie into borrowing my stuff and arrange the cave as the return point. You didn't know anyone was following you, and you guys left a clear trail to follow. Besides, you were using my map. I could figure where you would spend your nights, and I was watching when you returned from the summit. I just kept following you. Since you are the smallest, you became my target. Then you found all those strange things on the path and you put that stupid piece of armor on."

Janna had resolved not to favor him with a single word, but his last remark forced out a startled "What?"

"You know! That thing you wore that protected your heart."

"I know what thing you're talking about"—she snorted—"but what difference did that make?"

Philip Conner shook his head. "I couldn't let you make a single sound that would alert the others. You were often angry and went off by yourself, so getting you alone wouldn't be the problem. But the drug I got from my friend, who has the upstairs apartment in my building, only works quickly enough if you shoot it directly into the heart. I practiced blowing this needle through this tube every time you kids stopped for a rest. I got real good, but I couldn't do anything as long as you had that contraption on.

"You were really getting me worried. I sure didn't think you'd leave it on all day—especially the way you were always complaining about it." He rubbed his hands together. "Now everything's back on schedule. When your friends wake up, they'll find your piece of junk and a note with my demands. If they care for you, it won't be long before you'll be seeing them again."

Janna questioned, "But why are you doing this? We're just kids. What did we ever do to you? What kind of demands are you asking?"

Philip shook his head. "You just don't understand, do you? You've had it so good, protected from everything in that Dome. I'll bet your dad is real good to you too. Well, I'm going to prove to my dad that I'm not a failure. When I'm rich and famous, he'll see. And when he comes with his hands out, I'll turn him away with great joy. He'll see!"

Juli found the breastplate and note as she went looking for her absent sister and decided to check the latrine. She ran back up the trail. When the trio had absorbed what was written on the note and who had written it, they could only stare at each other.

"Apparently, he didn't believe we would come back like we said. Now, I wouldn't give him the time of day. Boy, Janna had better be okay!" Darcie looked fierce.

Josh paced around. "I can't believe he'd do something like this. We trusted him. I liked him. How dare he!"

Having used his helmet as his pillow, Josh now tugged it on. "Let's do something. After all, he thinks we're just kids. Let's go after him." He drew out his map. "Look, here's a forest near the cave where we agreed to leave his stuff. Of course, he won't be waiting at the cave, but he'll probably be close. I'll bet he has a camp in that nearby forest. I'm going looking for it. You guys wanna come with me, or would you rather go to the cave like the note says?"

Juli touched Josh's arm. "We'll go with you, but if you can't find him quickly, then we need to get to the cave. The main thing is to get Janna back, safe and soon."

Darcie and Juli drew together as Josh started breaking camp and began stuffing their things helter-skelter into any bag.

Juli spoke softly to Darcie, "Remember, in our dream, He told us that He could hear us anywhere? Let's try it and see if He can help us now."

Darcie agreed, so Juli, not quite knowing what to say and where to face, stood facing Darcie and then just recited aloud the situation they were in and then concluded with a plea for help and guidance.

Her final words of "Thank you" seemed to still be echoing in the air when Darcie said, "That sure made me feel better! C'mon, let's help Josh pack. We might have some kind of plan by the time we get to this forest that Josh is convinced is Mr. Conner's hiding place. Although how you find two people in such a large place is beyond me."

Josh was in the lead as they left the camp in the early morning light. Dew was still sparkling on the ground, and their feet became damp as Joshua guided them off the earthen path and across a flowering meadow. Hours passed, and the sun became hot on their faces. At least they were walking toward the Dome area, but they were certainly not on a direct path. It took them a couple of hours of hard walking, stopping only briefly to rest, before they reached the part of the valley where the small forest grew. They paused just outside the first boundary of trees, trying to peer down the overgrown yet visible path.

Knowing he had to continue yet not anxious to enter the dark growth in front of him, Josh remained posed on the barrier. Finally, motioning with his arm, the three moved silently toward the forbidding cluster of trees.

As the sun disappeared from above them, the forest grew dark and chilly. The trees had twisted and entwined so even the rays of sunshine searched for an opening. The trio crowded together as they walked along the eerie path.

Juli whispered, "You know, I haven't heard any birds singing and haven't had to swat at one insect since we've been in here. All I can smell is the same damp smell when Josh leaves his wet gym socks in the hamper."

Pushing through brush and pulling briars out of her shirt one more time, Darcie nodded in agreement. "I seem to be struggling for every footstep I make. Boy, it is really full of every kind of nasty tree and bush you could think of."

Finally, Josh called a halt in a small clearing.

"Look, I'm going on alone for a ways to see if I can find a path or something. You girls wait here, and I'll be back soon."

Without waiting for consent, Josh disappeared into the clinging foliage. Darcie and Juli moved to the center of the clearing and sat on the mossy ground, arms hugging their bodies against the damp and cold. At first they didn't speak then Juli asked, "Did we do something wrong?"

"How do you mean?"

"Well, you know, getting that encounter on the mountain and now this. I sure haven't gotten any plan to help find Janna. And I assume you didn't either or you would have said something."

"No." Darcie shook her head. "I don't have any ideas either."

"Exactly! So I just wondered if we missed doing certain things and that's why He doesn't answer."

"No, somehow that doesn't seem right." Darcie hugged her knees and rocked back and forth. "He didn't say anything about us doing something special. I just feel so calm about this. I mean, I'm angry and I want to do something, but it's kinda like it's already been taken care of. I just haven't seen the results. Does that sound dumb?"

Juli shook her head and replied, "Funny, but you know, it doesn't sound dumb. Although I think it should. I have the same peaceful feeling you do. I wasn't sure I should with Janna in trouble. Maybe we don't have a plan yet because Josh isn't back with the information we need. Darcie, since we have to wait and I really enjoyed the feeling I got when I was talking to Him, let's do it again."

Darcie readily agreed. This time, they joined hands, and a deep calm and quiet surrounded them as, one after the other, they spoke what was on their hearts. The damp air seemed to grow warmer, and their hearts felt lighter.

The sound of breaking branches distracted them. A tousled brown head appeared over a bush as a tearful Janna, followed by a grinning Josh, walked into the small clearing. The girls jumped up with surprise and happiness on their faces.

"What happened?"

"Oh my, this is wonderful!"

"Quick, tell us everything."

"This is great!" Words tumbled from the girls' lips.

Joshua strutted around the clearing while Janna fell into her sister's waiting arms and sobbed. "Oh, I'm so sorry that I disobeyed. I really made a mess of everything and caused a lot of bother. Please tell me you'll forgive me! I never want to complain again about anything. I must learn about contentment and counting my blessings. Oh, it's good being free! I really am sorry that you were forced to this awful place just because of me."

Words continued pouring out as fast as Janna's tears fell. The girls quickly hugged her and reassured her of their affection. Janna's tears slowed and a smile grew across her face as she experienced their forgiveness and love.

Juli spoke, "We belong together, and when one is missing, it leaves a big hole for the rest of us."

With Janna still sobbing (yet it was a contented crying), Darcie turned her attention to Josh, who still paced about.

"Well, tell us everything!" She prompted.

"If you're ready to listen now, I'll tell you what happened. It was amazing and I was very clever. When I left you, I found a trail, and it ended at his camp. Of course, I'm much more experienced with this sort of thing than any of you are since I had those camping classes and I could sneak real close.

"Janna was tied up under a tree, and that evil old man sat facing her working on some notebook. I could knock him out easy, only there wasn't a rock, limb, or anything I could use as a club. He seemed to have cleared out his camp of anything lying on the ground, and if I broke something off a tree, he'd hear me.

"I didn't want to leave my spot and look for something because I didn't know if he planned on leaving soon, so I crouched in the brush just behind him. Of course, I knew I'd figure out something, and then it just came to me that the helmet would make a good weapon. Although mostly leather, there is this metal piece on top. So I took it off and hit him over the head. I was so strong and right on target, and it only took one blow.

"Then I got Janna and brought her away safely. Now I'll lead us home and deliver the message to our people. I'm sure my special abilities are why He chose me instead of you."

As Josh talked, the three girls exchanged glances. "Oh, hold on a minute, Josh! Who do you think you are?" Darcie finally cried out, exasperated. "I don't think you are any more important than the rest of us. He gave us all gifts, remember? He told all of us to stay together and that we needed each other." A look of concern crossed her face. "Remember the things that happened when we didn't follow His instructions. Don't you go and do something dumb!"

Chapter Eight

BRICK BY BRICK

Josh's helmet lay on the ground close to Janna where he had tossed it while regaling them with his tale of rescue. He walked over and picked it up. "Look, girls, I don't have time for discussions. I'm gonna study the map and plot the fastest way out of here. Be ready when I am."

With his helmet tucked under his arm, Josh turned away.

"Josh, wait a minute!" Darcie called. "Shouldn't you put your helmet back on? Remember what happens when we put down our gifts!"

At first, Josh didn't answer; but as the silence grew longer, he muttered, "It doesn't fit anymore."

Juli leaned forward. "What did you say?"

In anger, Josh flung the helmet down on the ground and then kicked it. He screamed, "Because it doesn't fit!"

Janna ran over and pulled the headgear out of the brush. She hugged it against her chest. "But, Josh, you put it back on after you rescued me."

Tears lay at the edge of Josh's eyes and threatened to spill down his cheeks. "Yeah, I know. But while you were telling the girls how sorry you were and I was planning on how best to tell our story, it seemed to start pinching my ears and giving me a headache. So I took it off until you were done with your crying. But just now when I tried to put it back on, it felt like it had shrunk three sizes." He reached up and drew his hand across his eyes. "But I don't think it really matters. I probably don't need it any longer."

Juli spoke up with astonishment in her voice, "Have you lost your mind, Josh? Having that helmet, given for the use of us all, means you can't just junk it. Instead, find out why you can't use your gift anymore. The way you're acting, it's probably the size of your head."

"And just what do you know about it? I didn't see you rescuing Janna. I did! I don't see you reading this map, guiding us home. I didn't hear Him speak your name and give you specific instructions. You girls couldn't get anywhere without me!"

Darcie had been increasingly quiet as Josh spoke. Now she walked toward him until they were almost nose to nose. "Look, you are turning into a royal pain. You wouldn't even be out on this trip if you and Janna hadn't been eavesdropping. This was my idea, not yours, and I did all the planning. I let you carry the map because it got you off my back, but don't forget who carried the food we packed!"

Darcie's voice increased in volume as she lost control of her anger.

Janna, fearing a fistfight between them, dragged on Josh's arm.

Juli stepped toward Darcie and quietly asked, "Darcie, is this the way to handle this? Stop and think for a moment!" She reached out and touched Darcie's shoulder to draw her attention. "I don't think you should be doing this. Can you still feel that peace we just discussed? Do you still feel good inside? Don't think about whether you're right or whether he is. Stop! Now! Besides, he can't hear your advice in his mood."

Darcie drew her gaze away from Josh and looked at Juli. She focused in on Juli's words, and Juli watched Darcie's facial expressions map her thoughts.

After a deep breath, the elder teen took a step back and said, "You're right, Juli. Josh, I'm sorry. I still think that we are all important, but even if I can hit harder than you, that won't change your opinion."

Josh, obviously surprised with Darcie's change of action, still refused to relent and acknowledge her apology.

Janna still held her brother's arm. Now she gave him a little shake.

"Josh, come on. I'm on your side, you know. I love you very much, but you know you didn't tell the whole story about what happened when you rescued me. And it's like it's making you a different person."

"Shut up, Janna! I told what was necessary. You're safe, aren't you?"

The other two girls, listening, glanced at one another. Juli asked, "What do you mean, Janna? What didn't he tell?"

"Janna, I mean it. You'd better just shut up!"

"No, Josh, I'm not gonna shut up this time. I've always let your storytelling go before, but I don't think I can this time."

She glanced at the frowning face of her twin. "Josh told pretty much what happened, but he left out one part. You see, he knocked that old man on the head all right, but it wasn't really hard, and it only resulted in Mr. Conner groaning and holding his head, trying to get up.

"Then when Josh came over to untie me, he found the knots were real tight, and he couldn't get me loose. We were both so afraid Mr. Conner would be able to stop us before I could get free. That scary old man was still trying to get up and come over to us. A big blue lump was beginning to show on his head. But my legs being tied meant I couldn't even run. I remember that I was crying, and I kept saying that I wished someone would come and help us.

"Josh left me and was searching the campsite looking for a sharp stone or something that would saw the ropes off. I kept watching Mr. Conner roll around on the ground and make awful noises. I wondered who would get to me first.

"Just after Mr. Conner managed to make it to one knee and I'm screaming at Josh to watch out, I saw another man come out of the brush. Suddenly, I couldn't catch my breath and could only watch.

"The man didn't say anything. He walked over to where I was sitting, smiled down at me, reached behind the tree, and touched my ropes. They just fell off while Josh could only stand and watch. Then he grabbed me, and we didn't waste any time getting out of there. Now, Josh, you know that we'd probably still be there if it hadn't been for that kind man. He remained with my kidnapper—"

Josh's voice drowned out Janna's last words. "Oh, no, we wouldn't. I would have figured out something. So some man came and used his knife for a few seconds. I still did most of the work!"

Josh strode to the edge of the small clearing. "I'm done with this discussion. I'll find a quiet place and study my map, somewhere away from your ingratitude. I suggest you girls get a camp set up before it gets much darker in this forest. I'll set up my own camp and let you girls see just how much you need me. We'll leave early in the morning."

With those final words, he stepped out of the clearing and into the waiting forest, leaving the girls openmouthed with surprise.

"What has gotten into him? This isn't like Josh. Janna, put on your breastplate, follow him, and see if you can talk some sense into him. Darcie and I will start camp," Juli instructed.

Janna ran after him but soon returned. "He said he'd clear a campsite down the path so he won't be far away. Yet he said, again, that he wouldn't stay with us."

So Darcie gave instructions to set up their camp. She noted how they were able to work in accord, and not even Janna complained about the unpleasant tasks involved.

Occasionally, she heard Josh breaking up twigs and she saw Juli glance down the trail, once again hoping to see him coming with his arms full of wood. But the path remained empty, and Juli stayed mindful of the rift in their party.

Moments after he had dismissed his sister and ordered her back to the other camp, Josh shuddered. The swaying tree branches bent down and pressed around him, and he felt like eyes were boring into his back. The first thoughts of wild animals surfaced.

They hadn't seen any, although they had been warned by Conner that various-sized beasts were prowling the woods. Now, the girls had each other and the matches so they could build a fire for protection.

He had left the clearing without any supplies because it would have ruined his exit. Now he faced a cold, hungry night.

He could hear a faint murmur from the girls' camp. He decided he was far enough away for his pride yet still able to hear their voices comforting him in the otherwise still air. Using all the tactics from his manual to set up a campsite, he stomped down the grass in an ever-widening circle, broke off twigs on the small brush growing in his clearing, and moved stones to make a small barrier. One flat and somewhat smooth stone became his seat, and he pulled out his map and settled down for some serious study.

It wasn't long before the first whiff of food cooking drifted past his nose. His stomach responded with a healthy gurgle.

"Oh, that's just great!" he muttered to himself.

He bent even closer over his map as if that would make the smell go over his head.

Just when he thought he couldn't bear the hunger any longer and was even looking for an excuse that would take him into their camp, at least long enough for an invitation for supper, he heard the noise of someone approaching.

He quickly became engrossed in his map. feigning innocence of any presence. From the corner of his eye, he watched Janna push the last branch aside and stand in front of him holding an aromatic plate.

Apparently spotting her for the first time, he growled, "Now what do you want? I'm not going to help you in your camp, so don't even ask."

Janna replied, "Oh, no. Everything is set up. Juli fixed you a plate thinking you'd be hungry."

"Oh, well, that's nice. I just don't know that I'm all that hungry, but it will save time from having to fix my own. Uh, are you certain the camp is set up? What about the latrine?"

After Janna had glanced around, wondering what Josh had been planning to fix for his meal, she shrugged and set the plate down and turned to leave. Speaking over her shoulder, she answered, "No, really, we're fine. Darcie took care of most of your chores and found some water in a stream just north of you. Juli cooked, and I cleared the area and laid out our blankets. The fire's going, and we're just fine. See you in the morning."

Josh wasted no time in wolfing down the food, but it didn't taste as good when he remembered that they had managed without him. That was okay; he didn't need them either.

With the next day's journey planned out in his mind, Josh lay back on his grassy bed. Broken stubble poked him in the back, and grass tickled his arms like a thousand insects running up and down. He could hear an ominous rustling in the brush. He quickly sat up. Were those glowing eyes?

He knew if he wanted any sleep this night that he should make his camp more secure. He was in a small clearing completely ringed by bent and gnarled trees with dry-looking grass struggling up toward the blocked sky. With the clearing so small, the short leafy bushes draped over his bed, hanging in his face.

Looking around for logs or large stones he could use to make a barrier, he discovered a ropelike vine hanging from one of the trees. He tugged hard on the thick vine, and it fell at his feet. Each time he pulled, another fell with ease. He paused, wondering how they could fall so easily when touched yet remain hidden in the trees, resisting the tug of the wind that now blew in his face. With no easy answer, he dismissed the thought and quickly became occupied with applauding himself on how clever he was and how he'd show those girls a thing or two.

He tied one end of the vine around the first tree and moved in and out of the circle of trees, winding the vines back and forth and tying each around the trunks. There were so many vines and he had more than enough time on his hands that he continued to bend the vines around the trees until he had a fenced-in area of closely knit ropes. There was still enough room for him to crawl between the strands, yet he doubted that any animal of a size large enough to hurt him would find its way into his camp.

Now, the ground felt softer and the night seemed warmer. He curled into a ball; and despite the hard ground, the cool air, and the lonely feeling, he fell asleep with his clever thoughts for a bedtime story.

Josh turned his head and felt the warmth of the sun on his face. He rolled back the other way and tried drifting off again, but the sunbeam remained full on his face. Surely, it couldn't be morning already. Lying on his back, he decided he wasn't going to get ten minutes more now that the sun had succeeded in waking him. There was much to do today.

They needed to get out of this creepy forest and find the path that would take them home. So he rubbed his face, opened his eyes, and sat up.

The sun, which a moment ago had bathed him with warmth, now seemed hidden by a cloud. The glade was as dark and cold as it had been yesterday afternoon, and with the trees growing so closely together, he wondered how the beam had ever found its way to him.

His body demanded attention, and Josh had to make sure the girls were up and moving. He wanted his toothbrush, a body of water to wash in, and a huge breakfast.

Moving toward a small opening between the vines in his barricade, he sensed a difference. There was less room between the strands; and even as he watched, those gaps became filled with shoots growing together.

In astonishment, his feet remained rooted to the ground as, before his eyes, another section grew together. Suddenly energized, he raced the last few feet and bent over to wiggle through one of the last clear sections. But as quickly as he moved, it wasn't fast enough. The vines finished joining into a strong closely knit web.

Unbelieving, Josh circled the clearing, searching for an opening. He couldn't grasp what was happening. Perhaps he was still sleeping and in the midst of a nightmare. Any moment he would wake up and the day could start again.

But in his heart, he knew he was awake. After making several complete circuits in this trapping web of his own doing, he realized the barrier he had constructed as protection against being hurt had worked but not as planned. The hopelessness of his situation was becoming more apparent with each circle he walked.

Despair and loneliness reached out and gripped his heart. He groaned aloud from the pain, and his head sank dejected onto his chest.

The sound of leaves moving in the wind penetrated his mourning. He looked up. The vines were continuing to grow, and soon his small camp, covered by a mesh, would mean that he faced certain suffocation with the air replaced by green plants. Or perhaps the heavy vines would crush him if they started falling on him. He could not remain there!

It grew darker and darker as the vines climbed over his head, forming a canopy. In his first hasty search of the campsite, he found no tool to help. There was nothing on the ground. The small rocks he had cleared the night before, piled just on the other side of this living wall, could not help. He couldn't cut or hack his way out. He remembered the girls had the only matches, so he couldn't burn his way out.

The girls!

But of course, that would mean calling for help or actually screaming, since the foliage acted as a sound barrier. No, he couldn't risk that. Besides, what if the girls heard and ignored him? How would he feel if they laughed at his predicament? Hadn't he just told them that he didn't need them for anything?

Then sanity took over again. What was the alternative? He didn't have much time for a decision. He must take the chance!

Even as he wrestled with his pride, he spotted his helmet under a bush beside where he had slept. How had he not seen it before? Apparently, Janna had left it when she brought his meal. It seemed like an old dear friend, and he snatched it up. With it in his hands, a peace came over him. What had he been thinking of yesterday? He had broken up the team that the Eternal One had put together. He had wanted praise that wasn't his and had even lied to get it. When Janna wouldn't let him, he turned on her. He spent a cold night alone when he didn't have to. He ate bitter herbs for supper instead of warm fellowship. Boy, did he owe those girls a huge apology the next time he saw them.

On impulse, he clasped the helmet down over his ears, and it snuggled onto his head. His despair dropped off him like a cloak. He let out a might shout, "I need your help! Come quick!"

Almost immediately, Josh heard, from the other side, "We're here. We'll get you out."

With a catch in his voice, he cried out to the sweet voices on the other side of his prison, "I'm so sorry. You were right. I need you as much as you need me. Thank you for hearing me and coming."

Janna cried out, "It's so thick. What do we do?"

"Darcie, use your sword and cut a path towards my voice."

She answered, "Josh, it's not working. The vines grow back together faster than I can cut."

There was silence on both sides of the wall. The girls joined hands and were asking for a plan when Josh's muffled voice sounded.

"Darcie, the two cut ends can't touch again. As you cut, have Juli use her shield on one side and Janna hold her breastplate on the other. The wall isn't deep, just thick. I have my helmet on, and if you can get me just a small opening, I can force my way through."

He was right. It wasn't quick and the hole wasn't big; but Darcie cut, the other two girls pushed back with their equipment, and Josh put his head down and squirmed his slender body through. Finally, he was standing with them on the right side of the wall.

Again, the sun broke through the growth, and Josh smiled. "If that sunbeam had not awakened me so I could see the trouble I was in, it could have been fatal. Again, thank you for being there for me."

Chapter Nine

GOING HOME

I n a victorious mood, the friends packed their bags. They were going home, together and unharmed. Josh kept his vow and apologized to each girl individually.

A brief discussion revealed a common desire to return Philip's supplies as they had promised. Janna put their feelings in words, "OK, he's bad, but these items aren't ours. And we shouldn't break our agreement."

Josh spent a few minutes replotting his route, selecting the shortest trail to the cave. With a vast sense of relief, he led them away from the dark tomblike forest.

Back on the path for home, the sun grew brighter and warmer, and the air frolicked around them.

Following the map, the cave was quickly found. And it was there where Juli, sorting through the bags, left everything that wasn't theirs.

There was enough fruit and dried fish in Darcie's pack for their meals, but Juli asked Josh to find some water. She led the chorus as she said, "I long for a bath, hair wash, and clean clothes as I never have before. I will never take those niceties for granted again."

Darcie instructed Josh to get them as far away from the cave as he could in case their recent host, now turned enemy, came. "We just have no idea what happened to him after you left him with that man who seems to always be there when we need help."

Janna said, "I don't think Mr. Conner was harmed by him. I think we were just rescued from an evil action. But there isn't any reason to stay here. I want a bath—I need water!"

"Well, this path turns out of sight up here. Let's go that way and see what happens. It's along the path to home, although not the same way we've already traveled. According to the map, and if Mr. Conner was right, we're only about a day away from home. Let's get as close as we can because tomorrow is the seven-day rule, and we need to be within a few miles of the Dome."

Around the bend, the trail dropped down farther into the valley. Red and blue flowers lay as a carpet below them. The blue sky formed their roof, and fluffy white clouds drifted by, shading them from the warmth of the sun.

With the sky turning rosy, a slight roaring noise grew louder as Josh herded them down the smooth beaten dirt trail.

Juli pointed out the white birds that appeared from the direction of the roar and swooped down over them, as if checking to make sure the travelers below belonged on this path.

Ready to call a halt for the day, Juli clapped her hands as one of the white birds she had been watching glided to a landing on a large lake of snapping blue water.

At the farthest end of the lake was the source of the thunderous noise. A twenty-foot waterfall, much larger than the other one up the mountain, poured over the side of the cliff and tossed spray in the air.

Everyone whooped with glee. Janna set the pace as they ran over to the rocky shore and gazed down into clear water with silver-and gold-colored fish swimming and appearing close enough to her hands that she might catch them.

Trees, with long leafy branches, leaned over the edge of the stream that flowed out of the lake, and red birds sang a sweet song on the branches above. Red, blue, and white flowers pushed up bravely between the rocks on the shore.

As Janna gazed about, she noted two small thickets of bushes growing just to her left, with the stream on her right. The bushes acted as the walls for the clear patch of ground—just perfect for a campsite.

Juli, as she turned in a circle, voiced Janna's thoughts, "This is perfect. A place to bathe and wash clothes, bushes where we can change, a cleared campground, birds for music, and the sun for warmth. It's all we need."

Darcie shrugged her pack off and dropped it on the ground. "I agree. It's the perfect place for our last day out here. You know, it'll be great seeing my folks again. I admit that I've missed them, yet when we go in that door... Well, I guess I don't know what's gonna happen, but what if it's not the same, you know? I mean, we're not the same people who left on this adventure. I like myself better. What if they don't?"

"That's been on my mind too." Juli touched her friend's arm. "I think we should wait and see what happens and not worry about what could. Let's not be tempted to build scenarios." She glanced around at each face and added, "I'm glad that I don't have to walk through that door alone."

Darcie agreed. "We'll spend this final day out here, and tomorrow we'll carry out the mission we were given. Just wonder when He'll give us the answer. We're almost home and still empty-handed."

No one answered as this was on everyone's mind.

She watched, in the next hours, as, in silent agreement, they continued to enjoy this day together. With the ease of practice and without any prompting from her, the friends set up what should be their final camp.

She smiled, as one by one, the Turners jumped, clothes and all, into the deep blue water. She gasped as the first initial shock of the cold water hit her and then felt her body warm as she swam, dived, and tossed water at her friends.

Juli passed around the limited amount of shampoo, and everyone soon had clean hair.

Finally, Janna shivered and said, "My body is so numb that this isn't fun anymore."

She climbed out of the water and used the convenient bushes to change into her last clean, but wrinkled, outfit. She hung her wet clothing on branches in the late afternoon sun to dry. Soon everyone joined her on the rock ledge, watching the birds swoop over the water and climb, screaming, into the air again. The sun changed the color of the spray in the waterfall until the entire rainbow stood displayed for her enjoyment.

She sat mute, willing to spend the day in quiet companionship. She listened as, one after another, her fellow travelers retold the stories of the trip and laughed with them over events that didn't seem to have any humor at the time.

Juli fixed an early supper, and after everyone did their chores and the site was clean, the quartet sat around the blazing, warming fire.

The silence, not strained, was expectant. Darcie spoke first. "I feel like my heart could burst with joy when I think of all the special things that happened on this trip. Even the things that looked so terrible at the time turned out great. I don't know about you guys, but I feel I should thank the Eternal One for this whole trip and the way it has changed me."

Janna broke in, "Don't you feel like He's more than just the Eternal One to us? I don't think that describes all that He is. I wish we knew more about Him. I wish someone could come and teach us."

Her twin agreed but added, "He did tell us some things about Him, and so Darcie's suggestion is good. If He's listening, I think we should try telling Him how we feel about the gifts He gave us and how they helped us out."

Silence again fell until Juli spoke, quietly, respectfully, "Somehow, I feel that You are listening now—that You know every word I even think, not just the ones I think You should. I feel that You're everywhere, just as this wind is, and I long for more of You. I'm sure You know me better than anyone, and You love me more than anyone ever has, including my parents. I think that You were there helping each one of us when we were in trouble, and I want to thank You for the way You protected us."

As Juli finished her short monologue, they all became aware that, unconsciously, they had bowed their heads and closed their eyes.

Again, Janna first voiced all their thoughts, "See? He probably told us we could concentrate better doing this. So why won't He send someone who can teach us?"

Even as Darcie opened her mouth, Janna added, "Don't even say it. I know. I'm not sounding content again. Okay, let's just forget I said that. I agree with Juli too. I thank Him for keeping all of us safe."

Across the fire from Janna sat Josh. The flames danced over his cheeks and made his eyes sparkle. He had been listening attentively and watching the speakers. Now he stared at a spot over Janna's right shoulder. He started up from his rock seat, saying, "Hey!"

The startled girls looked at him, and he pointed. As one, they turned. A man stepped out of the trees and walked across the grass toward their fire.

Josh stood and watched. He glanced at his companions and saw no fear on their faces. Perhaps, like him, they only felt peace.

When the lone man was close enough, he stated, "Do not fear. I am a man of peace. I saw your campfire and came to see what was going on. Where are the rest of the folks? Surely you kids aren't out here by yourselves?"

Darcie's tongue felt glued against the roof of her mouth. It was almost like the encounter in town with Conner. Another grown-up was questioning them when they had no easy answers. With a smile, the man motioned them to sit, and she sank gratefully back onto the rock ledge. His smile turned into a grin that encompassed all the teens sitting in front of him.

"Are you the ones I've been waiting for? Are you from the Dome on the other side of this valley?"

Perplexed, Darcie answered, "Yes, we're from the Dome. But what do you mean that you've been waiting for us?"

"The same One who gave you your answer has sent me to help you. So here I am. I see you have your gifts already assigned."

Darcie and Juli looked at each other, and Juli's eyebrows almost disappeared into her hair as questions fought to be the first expressed.

Janna piped up, "What do you know of our gifts? Just who are you? And where did you come from? I don't see any houses around here."

The man nodded. "Good questions. Well, first, I don't have a home, at least here on this earth. I am a named fugitive by the authorities, so I have to live where I can. Right now, I stay in a small cabin I built in that clump of trees close to the waterfall. As for your gifts, I have one too." He drew up one pant leg, and the teens noticed for the first time a silver pair of shoes. It was not like a normal shoe but was made of finely beaten silver, was trimmed in gold with leather soles, and seemed to be melded to his foot like a second skin. "I am to be ready to spread the Good News where He sends me."

Josh leaped into the conversation. "So can you tell us what our gifts are for? Can you tell us more about Him? Can you tell us what happened out here that makes everything seem upside down?"

Juli laughingly quieted her excited brother. "Would you care for some food? Now, I know why we ate enough and still had some left over. Here it is, wrapped up and waiting."

The man grinned back and reached for the still-warm fish and two fresh apples, while nodding.

"Yes, I can answer most of your questions. Let's start with what's going on out here. How much do you want to know?"

Juli answered, "I don't know about anyone else, but I want to know everything I can about what has happened to us. I want to try to understand why we live in a dome and not out here. Someone out here was telling us about a civil war. I want to hear all you have the time to tell us."

"Okay." The man nodded. "First, let me introduce myself. My name is Peter Strong."

Josh quickly pointed and introduced his friend and sisters, ending with a thumb pointing to his chest.

Peter smiled at each in turn and then took a large bite of his last apple. "Years ago, the Creator of all this world became the enemy of some in this country who wanted their own way and didn't want to answer to a higher authority we call God. So they devised a plan and recruited people with a lot of money and found some lawyers to map out their strategy.

"First, they worked very hard to make anyone who followed God seem weak and incompetent, unable to make their own decisions. Then, they systematically began removing any mention of God from the learning arenas, public meeting places, and finally, from the very church that was to be the home of God here on earth.

"They used the argument that everyone had their own god to follow and should be able to do it in their own way so no one could prevent them from worshiping, or not, anywhere. They bribed public officials, passed laws, and finally, forced all believers in God to move into just a few sections of this country to live. They called it a civil war, but they were the ones with the guns. It was not even a war but a persecution of the way some in this country wanted to live.

"Some believers fought against being moved from their homes and businesses, and the government relocated those 'criminals' to areas where they often died in this 'war.' Others simply refused to move and were burned or shot in their homes. Many, carted off to a barren area just a few hundred miles to the east of here, died from disease and malnutrition. The land was hard and the water scarce and dwellings inadequate. A few, like my parents, went into hiding. As a boy, I have never had a place I could call home. We would have to move every few weeks."

At the sad look on Juli's face, Peter hurried to reassure her. "Oh, don't think I'm complaining. I'm just describing how it was. It was actually very nice. We met people who worshipped God and loved Him as we do. We would meet secretly every night and encourage one another. We never lacked for food or a place to stay.

"So that has been my life. God took my parents to the home in heaven He has prepared for them late last year, and I have continued their work, going where God calls and speaking the Good News He has given."

Josh spoke up, "But where do you get that good news? Does He speak to you? Is it written somewhere?"

"Good questions, young man. Here is the Good News, and it is written down."

With that, Peter pulled out a worn leather-bound book. Although small in size and looking like any other well-used book, Peter handled it as if it was of great value.

He passed it over to Juli, sitting closest to him. She thumbed it open and haltingly, in the poor campfire light, read, "'For I know the plans I have for you,' declares the Lord, 'plans for welfare and not for calamity to give you a future and a hope.'"

She glanced up at Peter. "Wow, that's great stuff."

He threw his head back and gave a hearty shout. "Oh, it's always so much fun to be around new believers. You remind me of the simple truth of these words, and it refreshes my heart."

Their teacher continued to talk long into the night; and Darcie, who had been sleepy as the fire warmed her, now wanted him to continue without regard for time.

Janna moved on the hard rock, not being uncomfortable but because she was straining to hear everything Peter had to say. She didn't have to swat at the flying insects that, earlier, had been intent on landing on her face—they were gone. Although the fire died down from time to time until Josh tossed another stick on, she felt no cold.

Juli asked where she could find a book like Peter had, and as he questioned her and a little of their lifestyle in the Dome, she glanced over at Darcie as they realized the book in their homes that was seldom opened and often dusted was the same book Peter referred to time and time again and could be their daily guide. Remembering every word he now spoke wasn't impossible because this book would state the same truths. She was determined to read and study it every day when she returned home, and those words would soon be a part of her life. And she knew her brother, sister, and friend would join in her quest for this knowledge.

Josh eagerly interrupted Peter's discourse and asked if his ancestors had been wrong to move into the Dome because the Dome locked the truth away from the very ones who needed to hear it.

Juli added, "We could have had our answer inside the Dome all along. We didn't need to travel out here."

Peter nodded in agreement and then responded, "Yes, that's true. But remember, even your culture has forgotten the great things

He has done and stopped teaching about Him. Time and time again, God has used human circumstances, choices, and natural desires to allow humans to make their own decisions and further His purpose. The place people choose to dwell does not limit His presence. Always it's the people's hearts where He dwells. He knows you better than you know yourself. He is your Creator.

"His love for His children is like this lake. You don't know how deep it is because you can't see the bottom. You can't know how big it is because you can't see the end. At times, like now, the lake is calm. But when the wind whips out of the south, it becomes turbulent, and the waves drive onto the land. However, there is always a point the water must retreat. You might like to sit beside the calm water, but the fishing is best when the waves pound the shoreline and stir up the bottom. He loves all His creation."

That statement caused Janna to ask about the fate of Philip. She pointed out that he felt he had the right to force them to help him achieve world status because the result would help them too. She asked, "How does he find the truth since he felt the end justified the means?"

Scratching his chin, Peter smiled and asked her, "Who was Philip Conner with when you left the forest? He will receive all the chance he needs to accept the truth."

Satisfied, Janna leaned back and smiled at her companions. Sparks swirled through the air as Josh bent over and laid a log on the embers of their fire.

Peter glanced around and asked, "Do you want to hear more? I could talk all night, but you do have a trip ahead of you and should get some rest. I have another small book that we give out to new believers to study on their own since we can seldom spend much time with any one group."

Reaching into the leather bag hanging across his body, he withdrew three cloth-covered manuals. Darcie took hers and thumbed through it. She noted that each day of the year had its own page.

Peter explained, "The words at the top are from the Bible, followed by a short sermon on the meaning and application to your life. Use this guide to supplement your own reading and discovery of God's Word.

"I, also, have this message for you. I received instruction to write it and seal it up and deliver it to the first four young people I came across. I'm under the impression you will know what to do with it."

Peter leaned across and placed a small sealed envelope in Josh's outstretched hand. Joshua said, "Thank you, I guess. But we'd like to know a little more about these gifts we've been given. Can you help with that?"

Peter nodded. "I was coming to that. You see, there are only two choices in this world, no matter where you live. You're either for God or against Him. For those of us who fight for Him, He has given gifts to help in our fight to bring others to know who He is also.

"As I said, my gift is to bring the Good News by traveling around and spending time with people, as I have with you tonight. Josh, you have 'the helmet of salvation.' You are to show the truth of God's Word to all who listen. We call people like that evangelists.

"Darcie, you have been given the 'sword of the Spirit,' which is the Word of God. As you study His Word, you will have a special understanding and ability to teach what is in there. You will have a great impact on little children. You will be a teacher of the Word."

Juli hugged her friend and waited eagerly for her turn.

Peter smiled, anticipating her unspoken question, and softly said, "You, Juli, have the 'shield of faith,' and with it you will be able to extinguish all the flaming arrows of the evil one. You will be able to distinguish the truth being spoken or the lies of the enemies. As such, you will be able to intercede for others, making you a great prayer warrior. You will spend much of this earthly battle on your knees, probably praying for the protection of your friends here."

Peter watched Juli's eyes alight with joy and a grin spread across her face. Finally, turning to the youngest member of the quartet, Peter touched Janna's arm. "You, my little friend, have on the 'breast-plate of righteousness.' It covers your heart and protects you from searing hurt. That doesn't mean you won't feel pain, but you'll be able to work in spite of it. That makes you a great missionary, one who can go into areas that not only need to hear the Word of the Gospel but also need practical help. You will often be in physical hardship, but you will willingly ignore the inconvenience.

"Now, these aren't the only gifts that God will give, and He will send others to help you along the way. But these are your gifts, and He will expect you to use them to help others find the truth of His love and strengthen them to walk in His light."

Leaning back against the rock ledge, Peter studied each young face sitting across the glowing, dancing fire. He wanted to share much more with them. Yet he knew that time and experiences would help mold and shape them into the spiritual warriors they would need to be to accomplish God's purpose. He knew it was time for him to leave.

He paused a moment to send a prayer winging to the Father's ear. "It's time for me to return to my home and leave you to finish your journey. God has given you a great mission and has protected, provided, and prepared you to bring the answer your home needs. Please wait until you're home to open the envelope. Would you join me in a final time of prayer before I go?"

Darcie, sensing that they would learn more about prayer from hearing this man talk to God, nodded her acceptance.

A short time later, their teacher shook each of their hands and, with a final grin and glance back at the campsite, took his leave. Josh quietly watched until the tree line swallowed Peter and the waterfall thunder seemed to swell in his ears.

Yellow sparks flew into the night sky as Josh tossed a final log onto the red embers.

The bright moon lighted up the camp area, and stars twinkled down on the group as a light breeze teased loose pieces of Janna's hair. She impatiently tucked the strand behind her ear.

She turned to Juli. "Where can I find instructions on how to become a missionary like Peter talked about?"

Juli, who had been very quiet for the past hour, patted her sister's hand. "Somehow, everything we need to know, we will know. Right now, we have just one mission: getting this message from God back to the Dome. I hope we will be able to find the right person to give this paper to and that the whole community will be able to hear it. I'm not tired, but let's try to rest at least a little. I'll bet it'll be a long day tomorrow. Don't forget, we still have to face the parents tomorrow. Boy, I'm not looking forward to that."

Quietly, Janna slipped into her sleeping bag.

But at first light, camp was swiftly broken. Joshua took the creased, slightly dirty, folded message from under the rock where he had hidden it and slipped it into his breast pocket. He checked everyone's backpack, adjusting Darcie's strap so it rode on her shoulder without causing a sore spot. Finally, he moved to the rock ledge that would lead them to the path home.

During the night, Peter, as their teacher, had warned the new warriors that many of the townspeople would reject the message they were bringing, but he reminded the message bearers they were to stand together and protect one another with their gifts.

Now, as they neared their home, Darcie suggested that they walk four abreast down the street, with the shield and breastplate positioned outside. She reminded her companions that while they were going to a home they were familiar with, the home was not familiar with them.

"Stay alert and ready for anything. We don't know the reception of our message. And don't forget the wrath of the parents."

Moving from the grove of trees, they regained the path and saw the Dome looming down the road in front of them.

Soon the shadow of the Dome framed their faces and the towering structure blocked the sun. The wind died to a slight touch, and the air seemed to drop in temperature as the sweat dried on cheeks and foreheads.

With a certain amount of trepidation, Darcie pulled the handle of the door and threw open the only entrance into the Dome. Side by side, the four walked into the familiar yet now curiously strange home.

There were many people moving about the streets. The travelers glanced around in surprise. Their once-quiet city was teeming with noise and congestion, and while it was a work day, many men were standing in groups and moving in and out of the surrounding buildings.

Darcie said, "Stick with the plan and head for the city building. We can call our parents from there and then deliver the message to the city council."

Unable to walk together because of the pressing crowd, Darcie led them on a weaving pattern down the street, moving toward their destination.

Behind her, she heard a young man holler out, "That's them, isn't it?"

Closer to her, several other young men turned and circled around them, pointing. One brave citizen reached over and plucked at Juli's shield and another tugged at Josh's helmet. The murmuring of the people closest to Juli became distinguishable.

"Look at them! Are these the children we're searching for?"

"No, they can't be."

"Look, their clothes are all wrinkled and have an odor. And they're carrying such strange items."

"Their skin is so dark and their hair is unruly and they don't look like us."

"Somebody call the city council!"

"Stop those kids! We don't want their kind here!"

The first rock thrown in anger in the history of the Dome flew toward Janna. Juli thrust her shield up, and the missile bounced harmlessly off.

After the initial silence of seeing a violent act performed before them, several more of the crowd bent and plucked up the small stones from a flower border trimming the lawn.

Before another missile could fly through the air, a path parted through the crowd as four city officials pushed through the mob.

One of the officials was the president of the Dome, and he waved his hands in the air and shouted over the crowd noise, "Just what is going on here? Have you people lost all common decency? We don't handle things like this! Have you forgotten our charter? Everyone is welcome."

With the appearance of recognized authority and order quickly restored, the crowd of mostly men fell silent and watched as their leaders cautiously approached the strange individuals they found standing on the path.

Josh, continuing as the spokesperson, faced the elders and said, "We are citizens of this place, like you, despite our appearance. We left here days ago, traveling through the badlands outside and searching for the solution of the mystery of the cold Dome. We apologize for the way we look. We only found a few places to shower, and we've had to wear the same clothes more than once. We've walked many miles, seen many things, lived in the open without shelter. But now we have returned with the answer sought by you elders. Our parents are the Manns and the Turners."

A gasp of disbelief went up from the listening crowd as Josh briefly related the trip up the mountain; the Dome dwellers stirred restlessly as the unkempt young man standing before them told of the experience with the Eternal One on the mountaintop. Angry mutters grew louder as he spoke of some of the truths they had learned on the return trek. When Josh reached the part of their journey where the teacher, Peter, had pointed them to the necessity of reading the Bib every day and how age should not be a restriction, another stone was lobbed over the heads of the closely pressed crowd standing around the quartet. One single word—"Liar!"—was hurtled along with the stone.

With alarmed glances into the crowd, the city council members, as one, surrounded the travelers and herded the young people into the shelter of the nearest building. Doors in the Dome never locked, yet the crowd remained out in the street, milling around and forming smaller groups of animated figures.

The president and one of the elders from the governing body took charge. John Luther ushered the young people into an interior room with bare white walls void of windows, with blue tile underfoot, and with a long table in the middle of the room where six chairs sat under the table's lip.

The president, Thomas Church, sent his secretary to find what area their parents were searching and to let them know their children were found and seemingly in at least good physical health. He ordered, "Tell the radio station to announce the search is over. Tell everyone to go return home and prepare to work tomorrow. We're way behind in our projects now after spending most of yesterday and today searching."

He turned back to the waiting young people. "It could be hours before your families get here, so you might as well be comfortable. We'll wait for them before we continue."

So the adults stood in one corner of the room talking quietly but doing a lot of gesturing, with the occasional raised voice quickly shushed. From time to time, one or more would leave the room only to return without a smile on their face. During one of the trips, milk and sandwiches appeared for the travelers.

The younger room occupants sat around the table arranged in the center of the room, stomachs in turmoil as they waited to see how their parents and these leaders would handle them and their story.

Juli glanced at her companions. "Are we sure this is what we're to do? I didn't think we'd cause all this commotion. I'm not sure this is the right way to approach the elders."

Darcie patted her arm. "Remember what Peter told us. Remain firm. We're doing God's plan. It's okay."

After a brief hesitation, Juli nodded. "Of course you're right. This is what we were called to do."

Just five minutes shy of an hour later, the steel door flew back with a rush of air and the mothers of the adventurers charged into the room, immediately overwhelming their children with kisses and hugs.

Even Janna's cheeks had tears making tracks in her dirty face. Over and over, she heard her mother say, "I'm so glad…so glad."

Behind the mothers stood the fathers, happy to see their children alive and well yet, from their glances at each other, knew their role in this affair had yet to begin. The bear hugs they gave their children spoke volumes of the pain that had been in their heart over the loss of their children, however briefly.

When the parents had finally reassured themselves that their children were home and safe and some semblance of order had been restored, the adults took the seats at the table while the children stood.

Josh, again the spokesperson, embellishing on the brief summary he had provided the crowd, presented their perilous yet triumphant tale.

At one point, Janna laid her hand on Josh's and he glanced over at her. At first, responding angrily and about to withdraw his hand, he looked into her eyes and relaxed. Turning back to the table of adults, he said, "I'm sorry, but I'm spinning a little more into this story than what really happened. Let me retell the part about Conner following us again."

Janna's mom gave many gasps of horror and gripped her husband's hand tightly time and time again as Josh reached the part about the kidnapping of her daughter.

Janna hugged her mom. "It's okay, Mom. I'm safe. I'm discovering that obeying the rules is good, and I'm going to work harder on doing that for you. Don't cry."

Darcie's dad rolled his eyes and muttered once, "Just wait till I get you home," but his wife shushed him.

Darcie grinned and said, "I guess the Z car isn't an option now for my birthday this year?"

Angrily, her mother turned to her. "What's it going to take to get you to let go of needing to be rewarded for everything you do?"

Darcie stepped back in astonishment at the anger she had never seen before. Biting back her initial response and seeing Juli watching her, instead, she nodded in agreement. "Yes, Mom, you're right. That is something I was shown I needed to work on, and with the help of God, I will be more giving and less taking."

It was her mother's turn to be startled. Yet after gazing at her daughter's open face and steady eyes, her mother nodded, touched her daughter's arm, and turned back to hear more of the adventure that seemed to have helped her child mature.

The tale, interrupted more than once with spontaneous hugs and even some laughter, concluded. The city council members, sitting at the table farthest from the young adventures, didn't look any happier with the second telling of the story.

Darcie's father questioned, "Well, what is the answer you brought back?"

Touching his pocket, Josh replied, "I have it here. I'd like permission to read it over the airwaves. We decided that all should get the message at the same time and decide for themselves what they should do."

His father questioned, "Do you kids know what the answer is?"

They shook their heads. Janna, sitting on his lap, said, "We thought we should wait and hear it with everyone else."

"But you're sure about the Bib and shutting ourselves off from the outside?" Her father shook his head. "That won't be easily accepted. You're talking about people changing their lifestyles and habits. We moved in here to deliberately shut ourselves off from the outside. I don't know if giving out that answer to just anyone is a good idea. We already have the makings of an old-fashioned riot outside these doors right now, and you're claiming we were wrong to move in here.

"Whether the Bib becomes easier for all to read or not won't be a major change for us to swallow. It might be nice to see it opened more often and even taught, but moving outside...I don't know!"

Juli, who had been snuggled in her mother's arms, spoke up. "Dad, we can't decide that. We don't have the right. Everyone must make his or her own choice, but we do know it's the needed answer. It'll explain why the temperature continues to drop. You must let us complete the mission given to us."

In the midst of heavy silence, the adults got up and drew together in a corner of the room. The quartet huddled together in front of the now-empty table.

Josh declared, "They're not going to let us do it. Plan B goes into action just as soon as they pull rank. Okay?" His companions nodded in agreement.

In one accord, they joined hands, and eyes were briefly closed as they silently prayed. Josh straightened his stance as he heard the parents and the civic leaders return to the table.

Josh's father stood behind his son and placed his hands on his son's shoulders. "I want you to know how happy we are that you're all safe. Ever since the camp called to confirm your registration for a week after you left home, we've had quite a stressful last couple of days. You, also, have had quite an experience, and we expect it'll take some time for you to settle back into a routine. So even though learning center starts next week, we'll give you an extra week's vacation."

He paused, waiting for a reaction, but the young people continued standing quietly.

Darcie's dad took over the narration. "We're asking that you turn that slip of paper over to us, and the president will lock it in the safe. The council will bring it up in their next meeting in about three weeks. All the elders will be there, and they can decide how to handle this.

"We don't think it wise to share your story with anyone else. You know, we can't be wrong in how we live because we've been doing it for several generations. If it was good enough for my dad, it's good enough for me and for you too."

His voice had risen in pitch and volume. His wife reached over and patted his hand. "Now, now, don't get excited. Remember what the doctor said."

He brushed her off impatiently. "Yeah, yeah. Darn fool girl, anyway—always getting in trouble." He turned and shook his finger under Darcie's nose. "I should have spanked you years ago."

His comment touched off a variety of remarks from the people present, and soon everyone was airing his opinion whether anyone listened or not. During this chaos of adult conversation, Josh pointed to the door. Quietly, the objects under discussion slipped from the room.

The events from their trip had taught them much, and they knew that it had been no accident that the mob had forced them into this particular building for protection.

Janna pointed to the logo on the wall and giggled. "Look, we're at the radio station, the very place we asked them to take us."

Josh pulled her arm. "Come on, here's the studio door. Let's go."

Behind Joshua, they marched through the heavy door, where the "On Air" sign was lighted up. The lone occupant in the room broke off his speech in surprise at the interruption but then gleefully spoke into his microphone, "Hold your phone calls! Those kids just walked into my studio. Perhaps we can get them to say a few words?"

Without hesitation, Josh walked over to the empty guest chair positioned across from the broadcaster. The man reached over and flipped a button on the microphone standing on the counter between them.

Josh, not wasting time for introductions, immediately began. "I don't know how long they'll let me speak, so I won't waste time. I have the answer about the cold Dome, and I was told it'll require a personal decision from each of us."

The sound of ripped paper was heard over the tuned-in radios, and the envelope was torn open. Then the quiet voice of Josh vibrated across the air. "The answer is…"

The studio door banged the wall as it burst open and the president hurried over to where Josh was sitting. Thomas Church reached for the microphone switch.

"Cold hearts!"

The End

ABOUT THE AUTHOR

Linda was born in Upstate New York, in the foothills of the Adirondack Mountains. Growing up on a thousand-acre dairy farm with six sisters, they were busy. She has always had a great love of fiction books and would consume them by the bookshelf.

After her marriage, her husband was sent to Vietnam by the Army; and upon his return, they were stationed at Fort Riley, Kansas. Their love for the state and their conservative values, along with great hunting and fishing, kept them here.

This plot became a focus of her life for a season, and she has drafted and polished the manuscript for years, enjoying afresh each revision. She prays that you will enjoy it too.

CPSIA information can be obtained
at www.ICGtesting.com
Printed in the USA
FSHW012322091219
64837FS